Last Known Whereabouts

By Margaret Riddell

Also by Margaret Riddell

Wolf River

◆ FriesenPress

Suite 300 - 990 Fort St
Victoria, BC, Canada, V8V 3K2
www.friesenpress.com

ISBN
978-1-4602-7401-9 (Paperback)
978-1-4602-7402-6 (eBook)

1. Fiction, Mystery & Detective

Distributed to the trade by The Ingram Book Company

Thanks to:
Ken for his good-natured support,
Pip for her patience and expertise,
And to Red, my chief motivator.

The Bystander Effect

*Through numerous studies, psychologists have
found that bystanders are less likely to intervene in
emergency situations as the size of the group
increases.*

*The presence of others makes one feel
less personally responsible for responding to events
and each additional person present lowers the
chances of anyone helping at all.*

*People tend to assume that someone else will provide
the necessary help, especially when there are many
others around who could potentially do so.*

*Latane, B., & Darley, J.
Bystander "Apathy", American Scientist, 1969*

Part One

chapter 1
The Door

The violent summer storm blew up without warning and the woman realized with panic that she had forgotten to close the garage door. She stumbled out into the garage and slapped the remote control button on the wall in the same instant as a crash of lightning killed the electricity. She hesitated for a short moment. She knew what to do; he had shown her once. She groped in the darkness for the flashlight she knew was on the shelf by the door. By its weak light she found the stepladder and dragged it into position beneath the manual release. She grasped the cord and jerked it loose.

No more than three or four seconds could have passed. But that was enough time for the woman to register the deafening explosion of lightning, the sudden sharp outlines and shadows of rows and piles of packing boxes lining the garage, and the blue-white illumination of the sheeting shards of rain in the open doorway. In that same instant she understood the hurtling descent, slow in its horror, of the heavy cedar garage door. She saw, silhouetted against the curtain of rain, the slow-motion dance of a child in an unstoppable quest to retrieve a ball that had rolled out into the storm. And in the last millifraction of the second, the thunderous crash of the door on the concrete floor shuddered the ladder upon which the woman stood. Her flashlight flew from her hand and landed somewhere between the dozens of boxes in the garage from where it threw grotesque shadows to the dark ceiling.

She half-climbed, half-fell down the ladder, missing the bottom two rungs and scraping both legs from knee to ankle. She screamed above the noise of the storm.

Baby! Where are you, baby?

Frantically she pried the flashlight from its trap and staggered through the obstacle course of boxes to the garage door. The lower part of the child's body lay at the bottom of the door inside the garage and the faint light of the flashlight revealed a pool of bright blood already blossoming beneath the tiny legs. The woman stumbled back to the ladder and felt for the dangling red handle. She clutched it in her fist and, hanging from the ladder, pulled with her entire weight. The door was utterly immovable. The flashlight fell to the floor again and cast an eerie horizontal shaft of light across the concrete. The woman pushed her way through the rows of boxes to the side door of the garage and stumbled outside and around to the front.

She knelt beside the child's unmoving form. No more than a minute had elapsed since the fall of the door. The pool of blood from inside the garage had already begun to leak under the thin crack at the bottom and was washing away, diluted in the sheeting downpour.

The child moved her lips, but could make no sound. The woman lifted the little head and cradled it and tried to shield it from the cold rain. *Everything will be all right, princess. Daddy will be here soon. He'll get the door up and everything will be fine.*

chapter 2

Most of the parking lots in Assiniboine Park were full because of the Canada Day celebrations. Janelle St. Clair found the last available spot in the long lot just north of the Conservatory. She and Nellie gathered their things and the Little Mermaid blanket (everything had to be Little Mermaid) and they headed toward the celebrations with Bobby Sperling the teddy bear tucked into the top of Nellie's yellow backpack. The majestic Pavilion towered before them with its dark half-timbering on stucco and the European-style roof. *Look, Mommy! It's a castle. Who lives there? Are there princesses?* Janelle laughed and hugged Nellie and remembered thinking the same thing when she was the same age and visited the park with her grandmother.

There was a small concession on the west side of the Pavilion and Nellie requested a stop for lemonade. They sat for a few minutes on a stone bench in the shade. *What's that funny little glass house, Mommy? Does it belong to the princesses too?* It took a moment for Janelle to realize Nellie was pointing to an old telephone booth. The telephone wasn't in working order and the booth was obviously just an outdoor museum piece. Janelle showed her how it would have worked in its day. Nellie was fascinated by the old rotary dial and she insisted on twirling in the numbers of their home phone.

They carried on past the vine-covered pergolas on the north side of the Pavilion. A crowd of thousands gathered for the Canada Day celebrations in the grassy wide-open area between the outdoor bandshell theatre and the Assiniboine River. Hot sunshine reflected from the river's barely moving surface. Nellie laughed. *It looks like a wiggly mirror, Mommy! A magic mirror for the princesses in the castle!*

A children's entertainer dressed in a wild costume of gold and red and green belted out ditties from the stage. They found a place near the front of the crowd where they could spread the mermaid blanket. Bobby Sperling sat on Nellie's knee, clapping his fat paws with Nellie's assistance.

"*Sandwiches are beautiful, sandwiches are fine, I like sandwiches, I eat them all the time...*" Nellie sang along with the crowd and waved her arms in the air. They stayed for three or four more songs, until Nellie noticed the little boy sitting nearby with his face painted like a frog. The quest was on for the face painters who were eventually found under the shade of a red and yellow canopy beside the theatre. There were several artists, and Nellie chose a young girl wearing a black and silver caftan. *So, what would you like me to paint for you? Do you see anything you like?* Nellie examined the illustrations. She giggled. *I don't know. There's so many pictures...* The artist studied Nellie for a moment, absorbing the blue t-shirt with the pink and purple butterfly on the front and the little butterfly locket at Nellie's neck. *Can I surprise you?* Nellie giggled and nodded. The painter worked with a speed that surprised Janelle. She produced a mirror for Nellie, whose reflection glowed with a sparkling blue butterfly.

It matched the colour of her new t-shirt and the swatches of synthetic turquoise hair in her dark ponytails. The butterfly covered most of Nellie's face and her eyes became huge dark spots on the wings. Her nose morphed into a purple butterfly body. The artist applied co-ordinating blue lipstick and handed her the mirror again. Impulsively, Nellie thrust Bobby Sperling toward the face-painter. *Can you do Bobby Sperling too?* Before Janelle could interfere, the painter took Bobby Sperling and studied the well-worn fuzzy red face. *Hmm. He's a very handsome bear. I might be able to think of something.* When she handed him back to Nellie a moment later there was a tiny silver star on the end of his black embroidered nose. Nellie was delighted.

"Wait a second, sweetie, hold still." Janelle focused the little pocket Canon and snapped a picture of Nellie and Bobby Sperling in all their face-painted glory.

Strains of *The Cat Came Back* rose from the stage behind them. Nellie's plan to return to the music dissolved when she spied an ice cream vendor. They made their way through the crowd to the waiting lineup. Finally the soft ice creams were in hand, leaking sticky chocolate streams down the sides of the cones and onto their fingers. A kind woman with long dark hair tapped Janelle on the shoulder and offered them a handful of tissues. Janelle found a place to spread the Mermaid blanket and they sat down to eat their cones. *Careful, Mommy! Don't sit on Ariel's face!* When they were finished Janelle pulled wet-wipes from her backpack and cleaned Nellie's hands and face, being careful not to disturb the butterfly. They walked back past the outdoor theatre, and Nellie zeroed in on the huge bouncy castle and slide over on the far side of the space. *Can I, can I, can I, please, mommy, can I?* Janelle's feet were hot and aching. *Don't you ever get tired?* In reply, the child skipped and hopped through the throngs toward the castle, Janelle racing behind to keep her in sight, sore feet forgotten. The crowd was a teeming kaleidoscope of summer color—yellow, blue, green, red, white. For one horrifying extended moment Nellie disappeared in the crush of bodies. The black and turquoise ponytails resurfaced a couple of seconds later and Janelle exhaled a deep breath of relief.

There was a long lineup at the bouncy castle but Janelle was surprised at how quickly they reached the tiny ticket kiosk. They stood in the queue with a family, a mother and father and two children—a girl about Nellie's size, the other one a little older. The girls wore twinned red outfits and had colour-coordinated butterfly faces like Nellie's. The pimply-faced attendant allowed all three girls in at the same time, after making them leave their footwear at the entrance. Janelle picked up Nellie's blue sandals and wedged them into the Little Mermaid backpack beside Bobby Sperling. She watched the girls disappear into a dark blue vinyl tunnel. Through smudgy plastic windows on the side of the castle parents watched their children falling and laughing as they navigated the inside of a huge, slowly rolling barrel. The barrel dumped them into a wide bouncy space where children flung themselves against the walls and tried to see how high they could jump. The children began climbing the padded stairs to the top of the slide, and Janelle moved to the slide area at the end so she would be there to see Nellie come down. A wide range of size and age emerged at the top of the slide. The older children, especially the boys, were fearless, pushing off to get a faster ride. The smaller children were visibly apprehensive. One little boy, younger than Nellie, sat screaming at the top of the steep slope. His father tried to talk him down but the child panicked and lost his grip on the smooth blue vinyl and sailed out of control to the bottom, still hysterical. The two sisters in red poked their heads over the top of the slide and came down hand in hand, shrieking as if they were plunging to their deaths. *Nellie will be next.* Three older boys made a rambunctious exit with a show of chest-thumping bravery. *Aren't you a bit old for this castle?* Time stretched before the next sliders—a boy and girl—appeared at the top, followed by a cluster of five, apparently a family. But no Nellie. Janelle stumbled through the watchers to the plastic window. Nellie was not on the bouncy surface. It wasn't possible to leave by the entrance because of the rotating barrel. The only way out was up the ladder to the slide. Janelle ran back to the slide area. Where were the two little girls in red? She saw them a short distance away and ran to catch up. *Do you remember my little girl? She went into the castle with you?* Yes, they remembered. She was right behind them when they started up the stairs. Janelle raced back to the window. She could see all of the bouncy space except for the far corner at the bottom of the slide.

She shoved and barged her way through the lineup to the ticket kiosk. *My daughter didn't come down the slide! Something is wrong*! Her voice was strident and raw. *My daughter never came out. She never came down the slide! She's still inside. She must be hurt*! The attendant gawked at her as if she had lost her mind and opened the gate to allow two more children into the castle. The parents of the red-outfitted girls joined her and the father took charge. *Can you get inside to check*? he asked the attendant. *How hard can it be? She never came out, she never made it to the slide.* Onlookers gathered. The father insisted. The attendant rolled his eyes and shut down the kiosk. He yelled into the blue tunnel, *Everybody out*! The crowd watched as children spilled down the slide. When it appeared the castle was vacant the attendant went around to the back of the castle. There was a small emergency flap-doorway in the vinyl wall, secured with wide strips of black Velcro and opening only from the outside. Janelle followed him into the enclosed space in spite of his admonition to stay out. They searched every possible nook and space. Nellie was not in the castle.

The parents of the two girls in red pulled Janelle away from the ride. She was crying and incoherent. The mother held her tightly while the two girls in red somersaulted on the grass beside them, oblivious to the crisis. The father pulled his cell phone from his pocket and dialed 911.

An assortment of law enforcement personnel—Winnipeg City Police, Park Commissionaires, and two plain clothes offi-cers—appeared on the scene within minutes. They taped off the area and tried to disperse the crowd to a distance of non-interference. Janelle and the helpful family remained close to the castle, along with the kiosk operator, who still didn't seem to register what had happened.

Within minutes, one of the police officers found a bright turquoise hair swatch on the grassy strip behind the bouncy castle. He showed it to Janelle.

She stroked the blue hair.

"Yes," she said. "That's Nellie's."

She felt a blackening in the air around her as she fell to her knees. Her purse fell to the ground and spilled its contents on the grass and under the feet of the police officers, and they gathered up the items for her and stuffed everything back into the bag, except for the little Canon camera, which had skittled across the grass and was lost in the feet of the crowd. Janelle barely noticed.

"It's all my fault," she whispered. "Just like the last time. All my fault."

chapter 3
Eagle Hill

It was happening again.

Everything was the same—the first days of panic, the endless rounds of questioning, the living room and kitchen clogged with police and detectives, reporters and friends and people out on the streets plastering posters anywhere they could find a flat surface, and news media beating the sparse clues to death. But Susan was gone. Just as Nellie was now gone.

It was Susan's face, not Nellie's, which now filled her mind. The circumstances of the day her four-year-old sister disappeared were etched in Janelle's subconscious like a dark negative image. Memories, repressed for years, began to unfold in detail in the wake of Nellie's abduction. Much of the recollection was inconsequential, but it was as inseparable from the unspeakable facts as is a shadow from a body.

And even after all these years, every detail rose to the surface and played out in photographic detail.

It was the last normal time in Janelle Carpenter's life. It was a family camping trip, the long weekend of August. Janelle's best friend Zola-Rae Thomson had been allowed to join them.

Zola-Rae was aggressively persistent in her pestering of Janelle's parents, Jerry and Yvonne Carpenter, and eventually they relented. Jerry was apprehensive about including her because Zola-Rae's presence usually meant that little Susan was ignored. Zola-Rae was a domineering child and Janelle was submissive. From Janelle's perspective, life was more exciting with Zola-Rae at the helm. From Jerry and Yvonne's perspective, Zola-Rae was not a good influence.

Jerry Carpenter chose thoughtfully from the map shown him at the check-in office at the Eagle Hill Campground north of Winnipeg. Like a little pig, Janelle rooted her head under his arm so she could see what he was looking at. It was important to satisfy Yvonne's specifications. The bored attendant yawned at his questions. Is it a dry spot? *Yep.* Is there plenty of shade? *Um-hm.* Are the showers close by? *No problem, man.* Jerry and Janelle settled on a site on the north side of the camping area and Jerry paid with cash.

It wouldn't really have mattered where the campsite was situated. Yvonne Carpenter was rarely satisfied with anything. She waited in the car with four-year-old Susan, who was her favourite, and Zola-Rae who was pouting because she was not allowed to go to the check-in office. Jerry and Janelle returned to the car and Yvonne snatched the map from Janelle's hands. She studied it for all of ten seconds.

"Why on earth did you pick one so far away from everything?"

Jerry winked at Janelle. "We thought it looked like it had everything we needed, didn't we, Jannie?"

Yvonne shoved the map back at Janelle. "We'll see."

They located the site, number 47, and Jerry backed the car in. The area was slightly elevated, shaded by gnarly burr oaks and trembling aspen, and larger than the nearby sites. It was just a short walk on a good path to the water tap and toilets. Yvonne stood with her arms folded across her chest while Jerry unloaded everything from the trunk onto the ground. He refused to look at her.

She slammed the drink cooler and Coleman stove onto the picnic table and kicked the rolled-up ground sheet through the dust towards the spot chosen by Jerry for the tent.

"What's the matter with you?" he asked.

"What's the matter? Everything. You should have let me look at that map before you made a decision on a site."

"Well, as I recall, you refused to get out of the car to come in to the office."

She didn't answer.

Janelle could still picture him as he contemplated the smooth fine gravel, the strip of grass to one side, the sun filtering though the tall shade.

"What's wrong with it?"

"For one thing, Jerry, it's just about as far away as you could possibly get from the lake and everything else. It's isolated. The toilets and showers are too far away. The bush will be full of mosquitoes and there won't be any sun in here in the afternoon. What the hell were you thinking?"

"For God's sake, Yvonne, it isn't that bad. Anyway, it's only for two nights. And I can drive the girls down to the lake if they can't walk that far."

He took a deep breath and turned to the tent which lay partly unfolded on the blue tarp. "Could you give me a hand here, Yvonne?"

Her too-loud voice carried in the still air. "I'm busy. Get the girls to help."

Janelle and Zola-Rae were both eleven. They were exploring the nearby pathways but could clearly hear the ongoing squabble at the campsite.

"Let's go back and help Dad," said Janelle.

They handed tent pegs to Jerry and did their best to pull the ropes tight as he asked. Susan, used to playing alone, retrieved her Barbie doll and her purple blanket from the back seat of the car and sat on the grassy strip in the shade, swatting at mosquitoes.

Yvonne threw suitcases and food boxes and air mattresses and bedding and lawn chairs into a pile on the gravel. She found the white plastic water jug and stomped off down the trail. Janelle and Zola-Rae giggled. They were always entertained by Yvonne's over-reactive antics.

When the tent was more or less stable, Jerry placed the mattresses and suitcases inside and put the food box on the table beside the cooler. Yvonne returned with her water jug. She supervised silently and disapprovingly as Jerry built a fire in the pit. He laid out the makings of hot dogs on the table and he could hear the girls laughing and crashing through the bushes in search of sticks for the wieners. Jerry unloaded the bikes from the top of the car and parked them behind the tent.

After lunch, a thin stratum of cloud dissipated the rays of the high-summer sun and the humidity thickened to produce a hot stickiness on the skin. The girls were pestering to go to the lake, so Jerry agreed to walk down with them. They were four bays away when they realized Susan had forgotten her favourite pink towel. Yvonne was already bug-sprayed and comfortably installed in her lounge chair with one of her new Stephen King books when they returned for the towel.

"Honestly. None of you can remember anything unless I spell it out for you." She found the towel and tossed it to

MARGARET RIDDELL

Janelle. "Tell your dad I want you back here by seven. Not a second later."

The next day adhered to the usual modus operandi for camping. Jerry cooked bacon and eggs on the Coleman stove while Yvonne set up the picnic table. After breakfast Janelle and Zola-Rae walked to the little playground at the bottom of the hill. Susan trailed behind, dragging her purple blanket and crying because they wouldn't wait for her. A little later, Jerry took them on a drive through the park while Yvonne prepared a lunch of sandwiches and watermelon.

The heat of early afternoon settled in and the girls clamored to go to the lake. Yvonne settled in her lounge chair. "You were there yesterday, you know the way. Get your swimsuits on before you go. And take Susan with you."

Zola-Rae protested. "Aww. Do we have to take her? We want to take the bikes. We can't take the bikes if Susan comes."

"Well, that's just too bad for you. It won't hurt you to walk. And make sure you remember to bring back the towels."

Jerry wasn't entirely comfortable about letting Susan go with the girls but there was no negotiating with Yvonne. He hugged Janelle. "It's okay, Jannie. You remember how to get there, don't you?" Janelle nodded. "And take good care of your little sister, okay? Make sure she wears her water wings."

"And you be back by five-thirty," Yvonne called as they disappeared down the trail. "On the dot."

Zola-Rae led the way around the curve of the bay. Little Susan, already falling behind, hugged her Barbie doll in her pink towel and followed the older girls into the pathway through the bushes.

It was just before six when Janelle and Zola-Rae arrived back at the Carpenter family campsite. The tall aspens quivered in a growing breeze and it was cool in the shade. Jerry's hamburgers sizzled and smoked on the grill. The picnic table was set with a checked cloth and blue paper plates and a rack of condiments. Yvonne lay in her lounge chair, bundled in her blue hooded sweat suit and covered with a red and yellow quilt. Slanted sunlight found its way through a gap in the low branches of an oak tree and shone through a pitcher of orange Kool-Aid.

This is the scene that was indelibly etched on Janelle's brain. This was what her eyes were seeing when, for the first time, the realization slammed into everyone. Susan was missing.

And now, Nellie is missing. Janelle knows she should be replaying Nellie's last moments as she entered that bouncy ride at Assiniboine Park. Instead, her mind can only evoke a vision of a sun-sparkled pitcher of orange Kool-Aid. It is the starting point of her recollection. It rolls out before her now, in high-definition wide screen.

Zola-Rae lines up Janelle and Susan behind her and dances the procession of three around the corner of the campsite bay and into a well-cleared trail through the bush. A small wooden sign with an arrow points the way to the swimming area. The trail is actually part of a network of deeply-shaded pathways connecting several bays. They all look the same, but signs along the way continue to give direction to the lake and to mark the location of different bays. Poplar. Sunset. Pine. Eagle. Their bay is Aspen, the furthest one from the main entrance of the campground.

"I'm the leader," Zola-Rae calls to Janelle and Susan. "Follow me!"

She hops on one foot, runs backwards, zig-zags, and spirals along the pathway. Janelle obediently manages to keep up but Susan falls behind and they can hear her crying. Janelle waits for her. Susan's Barbie doll has fallen out of the folds of the pink towel and they have to go back and hunt for it. Zola-Rae is around a curve ahead, out of sight. Janelle takes Susan's hand and they run to catch up.

"Oh, you went back for the crybaby," says Zola-Rae. And then to Susan, "You'll have to keep up, crybaby. Or we'll leave you behind. Right, Janelle?"

Janelle drops Susan's hand. Zola-Rae stands with her hands on her hips.

"Right," says Janelle.

They move along the trail in accordance with the latest requirement: walk ten steps, run ten steps. Repeat. Susan, dragging her pink towel, falls farther behind. She calls out. *Wait for me, Janelle. I can't see you.* Janelle stops, torn between her sister and her friend.

"You're not a sissy too, are you?" Zola-Rae frowns. "Oh, come ON. She'll go back to the tent. It's hardly any way at all. She can find her way back."

"Dad and Mom will be really mad."

"No they won't. They'll be glad to have their little sissy-baby back with them. Your dad didn't want her to come with us, anyway."

Janelle stands motionless. She can still make out Susan's voice. The crying is becoming more distant. It fades to nothing.

Zola-Rae skip-hops ahead and stops. "See? You can't hear her any more. She went back."

Janelle strains to listen. There is nothing but the chatter of overhead birds and the sound of unintelligible conversation from a nearby campsite.

"Well, are you coming, or not?" Zola-Rae strikes her hands-on-the-hips pose again.

Janelle throws her towel over her shoulder and follows the leader.

The girls arrive back at the Carpenter campsite just before five-thirty; Janelle has checked her pink watch faithfully throughout the afternoon. It isn't wise to circumvent Yvonne's deadlines. Even Zola-Rae knows this.

The scene is idyllic. Beatles music is drifting from Jerry's tape player, which is plugged into the car. *Ob-la-di, ob-la-da, life goes on…* Jerry is cooking hamburger patties on a grill over the open fire he has built in the iron-box fire pit. A lazy smoke rises from their sizzle. Yvonne is curled up on her lounge chair, her book upside down on her lap. She is dressed in a light-blue sweat suit and wrapped in the old red and yellow camping quilt. She is pretending to shiver in the light breeze. The picnic table is decked out with a red-and-white checked plastic cover and blue paper plates are arranged in five settings. The rays of the late afternoon sun cut through the branches and shine through a pitcher of orange Kool-Aid.

In that perfect, beautiful moment Jerry looks up from his hamburgers and registers that Janelle and Zola-Rae are alone. "Where's Susan?"

His words hang in the air for the split second it takes for the question to be absorbed.

Yvonne bursts from her chair, sending the red-and-yellow quilt flying. Her book falls to the ground and she steps on it, crushing it into the gravel. She repeats the question. "Where's Susan? Janelle, where is Susan?"

Janelle is mute with the horrifying realization that Susan didn't return to the campsite.

Zola-Rae steps forward. "She changed her mind. She didn't want to walk to the lake. She wanted to come back here," she says, unblinking. "So we brought her back to the road. Janelle even walked her to the curve so she could see your car. Didn't you, Janelle?"

Janelle nods at the lie.

Jerry and Yvonne run into the roadway. Yvonne is screaming. "Susan! Susan! Answer Mommy! Where are you?"

Jerry tries to take her arm. "It's been three hours since they left, Yvonne. She could be anywhere."

Yvonne shoves him away and crashes down the trail, yelling and calling. A few campers straggle from their sites and approach Jerry and the girls. No one has seen a little girl with a pink towel and a Barbie doll.

"You girls stay right here by the tent in case she comes back," Jerry yells. He jumps into the car and speeds down the access road to the park gate to get help.

The girls sit at the picnic table. Janelle is crying, and Zola-Rae pulls her close. She whispers fiercely, "You can't ever, ever tell that we left her to go back by herself, Janelle." Her fingers dig into Janelle's arms. "Promise, Janelle. Cross your heart and hope to die, stick a needle in your eye."

In the moment, Janelle hates Zola-Rae. *It wasn't we. It was you. I wanted to wait for her. Daddy told me to take good care of her.*

She extricates herself from Zola-Rae's grasp. "I promise. Cross my heart and hope to die, stick a needle in my eye."

By the time Jerry arrives back at the campsite with three park attendants, Yvonne has emerged from the bushes. Her face and arms are scratched and blood-streaked and her blue sweat suit is covered with burs. She is frantic and incoherent with panic, her voice hoarse from calling Susan.

The park superintendent assembles a small search crew and along with Jerry they systematically comb the pathways in the north section of the campground. Zola-Rae and Janelle follow them but are quickly sent back to the campsite and ordered to stay there with Yvonne, who is hysterical, babbling, and unable to move. The searchers find nothing, and decide to recruit three more attendants and some of the neighbouring campers to help. The search branches out to include the northwest and east sectors of the campground. By eight-thirty the bush and forest of the park have begun to suck in the late-day rays of the sun and the shadows are dark and deep. They are forced to call off the search for the day.

The park superintendent has called the RCMP, and they arrive at nine to deal with the Carpenter family. Jerry and Yvonne refuse to leave their campsite, and the park extends their reservation, free of charge. Zola-Rae's parents are called to come and pick her up, much to her displeasure.

The pitcher of orange Kool-Aid still stands on the picnic table. The sparkling light is gone from the prism of the glass, replaced now with twilight murk. A dying wasp struggles on the surface of the liquid.

The organized search was massive. It continued for two weeks, eventually stretching far beyond the boundaries of the park. The only clue to Susan's disappearance was the discovery on the third day of the pink towel, dirty and matted with burdock, over a mile east of the campsite. Foul play was a distinct possibility, and investigators diligently followed leads from as far away as Vancouver.

At the end of the third week of August, the Carpenters were forced to break camp and return home to their bungalow on Belvidere Street in St. James. Police and investigators continued their presence with an almost daily onslaught of questions and barren updates.

Every weekend until the onset of winter Jerry drove back out to Eagle Hill and searched for Susan. Yvonne went through the motions of living. She was consumed with creating posters featuring Susan. Every day she took an armful of her handiwork and plastered the posters on hydro poles, fences, bulletin boards—wherever she could find a naked space—in an ever-increasing radius of the city. Every night she found a different photo of Susan and generated another flyer and took it to QwikPrint to get copies for the next day's rounds.

Unspoken blame was thick in the household and Janelle could feel it, dark and heavy and cold.

Janelle was grateful, oh so grateful, for the small mitigating mercy of Zola-Rae's lie.

The following April, as soon as the snow melted and the ground thawed, Hank Oldman opened up his gravel pit south of Eagle Hill. He readied his backhoe to make the first cut of the season, and directly in front of the machine he saw the muddy Barbie doll. Its yellow hair was skewed with dirt and the once-sparkling red dress poked out of the wet muck of the pit. Next to the doll lay a sad little body, partly covered by a small slide of gravel under a slight overhang at the far edge of the pit. Susan Carpenter was six miles from the family's campsite at Eagle Hill.

It had been eight months since her disappearance. The coroner ruled her death accidental, from exposure.

Jerry Carpenter was a travelling salesman for Master Interiors, in charge of all wholesale flooring. In this capacity he had to travel throughout the province and into southern Saskatchewan and northwestern Ontario. He made one major trip a month, usually about ten days, to the west or east, and then several smaller jaunts closer to home. He used to hate being away from Yvonne and the girls. But that was then.

After Susan's disappearance and the discovery of her remains, Jerry's work became his refuge. Out on the road, he was able to put the awfulness of Susan's empty bedroom with its pink and purple frills and piles of tiny stuffed toys to the back of his mind. He could forget about the piles of "missing" posters throughout the house—posters that Yvonne would not allow Jerry to dispose of, as if she still somehow believed there was hope beyond the black cloud of her suffocating depression. His efforts to persuade her to go for counselling were futile.

Janelle existed, guilt-eaten, in the vacuum between Jerry's trips and Yvonne's depression. When Jerry was home, life was bearable; the rest of the time Janelle's only place of comfort was school. She was a good student and her teachers were sympathetic and supportive. And of course she still had Zola-Rae, who was her rock.

The incident with Susan was never spoken of, but it was always present, hovering over them like a dark bird that might, one day, learn to speak.

Just before Christmas that year, Yvonne disappeared. Her sister Marie called Jerry to let him know Yvonne had made it to Vancouver on the bus and had moved in with her. Temporary, she said.

chapter 4
Investigation

They considered that she might be complicit in the abduction. Janelle understood this, of course. In cases of disappearance family members were often the first suspects.

Jerry Carpenter sat beside Janelle on the sofa with his arm around her shoulder. Her best friend Zola-Rae perched on her other side and held her hand. Janelle hugged Bobby Sperling, the red teddy bear, tight to her chest. Her mother-in-law Nordeen St. Clair paced back and forth from the kitchen to the living room.

"You don't have anything to worry about, Janelle," Zola-Rae said. "This's just something they have to get out of the way."

"Just answer as best you can," Jerry added. "Everything you can remember. Just take your time, Jannie."

The officer sat across from them with his notebook, clicking his pen annoyingly. Nordeen stood behind him with her arms crossed.

"So, Janelle, if you could tell us everything you remember about Nellie's disappearance?" he began. "Even the smallest thing could be important."

"Where do you want me to start?" It sounded clichéd; she heard that the moment she said it.

"How about at the beginning?" That sounded clichéd as well. Janelle had the feeling of being in the middle of an episode of Law and Order.

"Start at the beginning of the day, and work your way forward from there."

"We were at the park for the Canada Day celebrations…"

"That would be Assiniboine Park?"

"Yes. It was just after lunch, and we parked by the Conservatory and walked over to the area by the stage where the entertainment was."

"Did you go straight to the stage? Any stops along the way?"

"We stopped for a lemonade at the Pavilion."

"Anything else? Did you happen to notice anyone questionable?"

"No. Nobody. After the lemonade we went right to the stage. Nellie could hear the singing and she was in a hurry to get there. We sat on a blanket close to the front of the crowd. Nellie was singing along and clapping…"

"How long were you at the stage?"

"I'm not sure. Five or six songs. Maybe fifteen minutes?"

The officer took several minutes to compile his notes and consider them. The silence was uncomfortable. He looked up.

"Did you see anyone close to you that might have been suspicious in any way?"

"No. It was just a bunch of kids and their parents."

He clicked his pen several times, wrote something on his notepad, clicked his pen again.

"Can you tell me what happened when you left the stage?"

Janelle's hand was cold and damp in Zola-Rae's. She closed her eyes and visualized the stage, the expanse of grass, the colourful milling crowd.

"Nellie saw a boy with his face painted like a frog, and she wanted to go and find the face-painters." Janelle touched her own nose and cheeks, trying to describe the sparkly artwork on Nellie's face. "She asked for a blue butterfly."

"Then we got chocolate ice-cream cones. And we sat on the Mermaid blanket to eat them. Nellie dripped ice cream all over her hands, and someone, I don't know who, handed her some tissues. Nellie wanted to go back to the stage, so we started to gather up our things. And that was when Nellie saw the bouncy castle. And nothing would do except that we go to it."

The officer was scribbling frantically on his notepad. Nordeen still stood behind him, hoping to get a glimpse at his notes.

Janelle continued. "I remember that I was getting a blister on my heel from all the walking we had done. I didn't want to hurry but Nellie ran into the crowd ahead of me. I lost sight of her for a couple of seconds but then I saw her just ahead and I ran to catch up."

"And by then you were on your way to the bouncy ride?"

"Yes. Actually it was quite close. It couldn't have taken us more than a minute to reach it. And we waited in line at the ticket kiosk with a mother and father and two little girls in matching red outfits."

"Can you remember anything about the mother and father?"

"Not really. Just that they were really good with their kids. Nellie struck up a friendship with the two girls right away. Nellie was like that, she was never shy with other kids. The three of them played tag around us while we waited in line. You would have thought they'd been best friends forever."

Then there were the final recollections of Nellie.

"The three of them went into the castle through a big blue tunnel. It was dark inside. The next time I saw her was when a big turning barrel dumped the three of them onto the floor of the castle."

"And you could see inside the castle?"

"There was a big plastic window on the side so parents could watch their kids playing."

"And you watched? For how long?"

This was the most painful part of the memory. It was the indelible vision of Nellie, laughing and bouncing, falling and rolling, and scrambling to her feet for more. It was the last time Janelle saw Nellie. She swallowed hard on the pain in her throat.

"I guess I watched for, maybe five minutes. Then it was starting to get crowded on the floor in there, and the three girls headed for the ladder that went up to the slide."

"The slide being the way out of the castle?"

"Yes. The way out."

"What did you do then?"

"I hurried around to the end where the slide came down. I could see the opening at the top where all the kids were coming out and I wanted to be there to see Nellie come down the slide."

"What happened then? This part is extremely important."

"I watched kids come down the slide and I waited for her. After a while the two girls she was with came down and I thought she'd be right behind them. So I stood there a few more minutes and then I went back to the window to see if she had decided to stay and do some more bouncing. That would have been just like Nellie. But she wasn't there. I went back to the slide, and that's when I realized something must have happened."

"What did you do then?"

Jerry squeezed her shoulder. "Take your time, Jannie."

She struggled to remember the blur.

"That's when everything starts to run together in my mind. I know I was yelling and calling Nellie. Everybody just stood there looking at me as if I was crazy. You know how sometimes you see a movie where they show everything in slow motion? I hate that, it always seems so phony. But that's what it was like. Everyone just seemed to be floating around me. Then I felt a hand on my shoulder and it was the father of the two little girls. He kind of took over, I guess, and got the guy at the ticket kiosk to close the ride."

"Are you able to describe the man at all?"

"He was tall."

"That's all? Think hard. Try to picture him."

"That's all. Tall. Very tall."

"All right. Tall. Then what happened?"

"The ticket guy closed the castle and yelled for all the kids to get out. Then he went around the back of the castle and I followed him. He told me to stay back but he opened a little flap and went inside the castle and I followed him in. It was empty."

"What happened then?"

"I'm not sure. It's still part of the blur. I don't actually remember it, but someone called 911. I think it was the father of the two girls. And the next thing, the police were there, and some commissionaires. One of the commissionaires stayed with me and wouldn't let me go back into the castle. And a few minutes later, one of the officers showed me a blue hair swatch. I knew it was Nellie's."

The officer continued his note-taking. "And what about the family...the parents and the two little girls?"

"I don't know. I don't think they stayed around after the police got there."

"So you didn't see them again? Get a chance to talk to them?"

"No. I don't remember seeing them again."

The officer flipped through his pages of notes. Nordeen still hovered behind him, glowering.

"So, that's everything?" he said. "Take a quiet minute or two and try to think if you might have missed anything."

There was nothing. Janelle believed every possible detail had been extracted from her memory.

The questioning then turned to Jerry and Zola-Rae and Nordeen.

Jerry had been at his little cottage at Lundar Beach on Lake Manitoba the whole weekend. This was quickly verified by his lakefront neighbours.

Zola-Rae and her husband Earl Bentley had spent the three days of the holiday shopping in Grand Forks, North Dakota and were checked in at Earl's favourite place, the Westward Ho Motel. Janelle's frantic telephone message had welcomed them upon their Monday night return.

Nordeen St. Clair was busy the entire weekend carrying out the organization of the Canada Day celebrations in Agate Hill. She arrived in Winnipeg early on Tuesday, the day after Nellie's disappearance.

It was in the early afternoon of the Tuesday following Nellie's disappearance that the 911 call was received. It was a very short call, less than a minute, traced to a truck stop just outside of Kenora. The voice seemed to be that of a child.

Several 911 operators analysed the recording of the call. All agreed they heard a child's voice saying simply, "This is Nellie. I need help…"

The little voice trailed away. There was no response to the initial operator as she tried to get more information. She could hear only background noise and the fading away of what sounded like a man's voice. Then someone replaced the receiver on the hook, and the call was over.

As soon as Janelle made a positive identification of Nellie's voice, the search shifted from Winnipeg to northern Ontario. RCMP took over the investigation.

Newspapers and television pursued the mystery relentlessly, turning it into a national story. The picture of Nellie with her red teddy bear was everywhere for weeks. Pleas for tips resulted in thousands of leads—but resulted in no solid evidence.

Zola-Rae appointed herself to be in charge of posters. She personally distributed hundreds of the brightly-coloured flyers all the way from Winnipeg to Thunder Bay.

There were virtually no productive leads after the 911 call. Nellie's disappearance was complete.

chapter 5
Erica

Erica Slesiuk had been a morning person from as far back as she could remember, and the early shift was her favourite. She wholly deserved her position as manager of Aunt Maggie's Truck Stop.

Erica would have made a terrible witness. Put her anywhere without a watch or clock and she had no sense of time or sequence of events. Her sense of direction was non-existent, except when she was shopping in the mall. She memorized landmarks to get from place to place. She never noticed what colour people's eyes were or how tall they were or what they were wearing; those things were just not important to her.

But seat those same people in a restaurant and Erica could take an order for two tables of eight at one time and never have to write down a thing. She could visualize the various customers in their positions at the tables and in the space of a few seconds, she imagined their lives, guessed their professions, pictured them doing everyday things, and heard their characters in their voices as they ordered.

If anyone asked her about the menu she quoted it verbatim, complete with recommendations and prices and possible substitutions. And if she met someone once, she never forgot their name.

It was July second, forecast to be cool and rainy. Erica had arranged to take the morning off, but there she was, at work. She preferred to have everything ready before the rest of the staff arrived, from the gleaming grill to the organized table-ware to the fresh flowers on each table. That particular day, it was snapdragons.

She checked each table, wiped a streak of dried ketchup from one of the dark green vinyl bench seats, and replaced the cardboard wedge under the leg of the wobbly table in the corner furthest from the door. She could never understand why the cleaning people wouldn't take the time to put it back after sweeping. She filled the napkin dispensers on each table and eyeballed the salt and peppers. The menus were a mess, breakfasts mixed up with lunch and dinner, some with their promo inserts missing. She sorted them out and put the breakfast menus at the front of the rack by the till. She poured herself a coffee and waited for her staff to arrive.

Billie showed up first and headed for the washroom before going to her kitchen. Erica could hear the familiar opening and closing of the cooler doors, shuffling of bags and packages. Billie was assembling her foodstuffs according to the breakfast menu, which Erica always left totally to Billie's discretion.

"What's your special this morning, Billie?"

"Thought I'd make a fisherman's breakfast today," Billie said. "Allen brought in a box of pike yesterday and they look pretty nice." No one could pan-fry pike like Billie. She was originally from Nova Scotia and cooking fish was her forte. Along with the pike she would serve her trademark hash-browns with chili and garlic, along with canned baked beans doctored with her

Margaret Riddell

secret ingredients. It wasn't a breakfast for the faint of heart, but the truckers loved it.

Erica printed the information on the menu board by the door—complete breakfast for four dollars, coffee included.

Kelly appeared next in the midst of a show of hurrying to get her navy apron tied on over her yellow tee and jeans. She was the front-line waiter and till-keeper.

Erica unlocked the door and switched on the fluorescent "Open" sign. It was five-thirty in the morning. The sun had been up for six minutes.

She was satisfied. She gathered her things and headed for the door. After all, she did have the morning off, and she had plans.

chapter 6
Finn Erikson

Finn Erikson's big semi thundered eastward on the Trans-Canada Highway, buffeting headlong into a thirty-kilometer wind. Finn's original plans involved reaching Kenora in time to entertain one of his favourite truck stop waitresses in his sleeper cab for a couple of hours, but a post-celebration hangover from a Canada Day party the day before now hindered him with a massive, bleary-eyed headache and a mouth tasting like used cat litter. Instead of arriving at the truck stop well before the waitress's shift, which started at eleven, he was barely past Winnipeg by then. On either side of the four-lane highway green oceans of wheat and barley unfolded in wide swells and surges that nauseated Finn, like a prairie seasickness. He stopped at the convenience store at Richer village to use the restroom. He splashed cold water on his face, then retreated to a dimly-lit cubicle for several minutes. The cool darkness eased his pain slightly. He grabbed two twelve-packs of twenty-ounce Red Bull from the tall cooler outside the restroom and bought a carton of Export A's at the counter. He downed one of the Red Bulls on his way out to the truck and opened another can for the cup holder.

Finn pulled out onto the highway and squinted at the horizon. The east wind was not good news, and he could already make out a darkening in the distant sky. There is no flatter land in the world than that of the Red River Valley of Manitoba, and there were few surprises in the sky. On the prairie, the approach of weather was visible in advance. Finn wished he had left earlier, as he had planned.

East of Richer, the farmland surrendered to the rocky outcrop-beginnings of the Canadian Shield—sandlands and forests of pine and tamarack, birch and poplar. Finn didn't love the landscape. He didn't hate it either; it simply didn't matter to him. He cared only about the conditions of the road and the potential for making good mileage. He drove cautiously. His load weight was well below the legal limit. There was no point in attracting attention.

Finn Erikson had worked ruthlessly and without conscience to reach his place in life, shaping himself out of his dismal childhood and the poverty of his upbringing.

Finn's grandfather Thor Erikson farmed in the southern part of Manitoba's Interlake and struggled to survive on a wretched tract of stony land where even the scrub brush was stunted. When old Thor died after years of relentless labour, having never managed to eke out more than a bare subsistence, his forty-year-old son Numi inherited the bleak acreage. The scruffy wild-grass pasture supported some grazing so Numi continued to run the small herd of nondescript cattle that went with the farm. Within months, he married Anna Kravek, the nineteen-year-old daughter of a Ukrainian neighbour. Anna was not a stranger to hard work rewarded by poverty and she toiled alongside her partner. In the first six years of their marriage, Anna gave birth to three children. Gunnar and Karl were followed by Elena, who was called Lynn. And six years later, Finnbjorn arrived.

Anna never missed a beat. Children at her side, she milked two scrawny cows and gathered eggs from her chickens and somehow coaxed potatoes and stunted vegetables from the gravelly garden. Anna always had eggs to sell, so once a month they loaded the family into the rust-infested pickup for a trip to Gimli to stock up on whatever supplies they could afford. Gunnar and Karl always rode in the back, huddled up against the cab to get out of the wind. Lynn got to ride inside because she was a girl and Finnbjorn nestled on Anna's knee because he was the youngest, and because he got whatever he wanted.

When Finnbjorn was twelve, Anna died of breast cancer. Gunnar and Karl were gone by then, adamantly turning their backs on the farm. They wanted no part of the stone pile, as they called it. There had been hard words with Numi; words that would never be forgiven. Gunnar landed a good job at the distillery in Gimli, and Karl worked at an all-season lodge on northern Lake Winnipeg. Lynn left too, heading for dreams in the big city with a questionable boyfriend. The last time Numi and Finnbjorn heard from her, she called to let them know she had given birth to a little girl. The boyfriend had disappeared, and she wanted to come home. Numi said no.

If, as they say, grief has several stages, young Finnbjorn Erikson never made it past the anger phase. He hated his mother for dying, and he hated his siblings for leaving. He hated his father for being old. And Numi was indeed old, far too old for his sixty-four years, weary and work-worn and defeated. But he loved Finnbjorn more than any of the others and the boy knew this. If he wanted something, all he had to do was ask, and Numi capitulated to every demand, no matter what the sacrifice. But Finn, as he by then insisted upon being called, always needed more.

Numi sent Finn to the pasture with the scraper one day to carve out a shallow grave for a dead steer. Finn scooped the carcass up in the loader of the tractor and headed to the far corner of the property where animal casualties had ended up ever since his grandfather Thor ran the farm. Finn lowered the blade of the loader into the stony soil and pulled it across the surface. Part of an old bovine skeleton caught on the edge of the blade and sprang upward from its miserable burial spot. Finn pushed the yellowed bones back into the soil and decided it was time for a new site. He loaded the dead steer again and headed for a high ridge along the fence line between the house yard and the highway. He set the blade down and was surprised when the ground gave way easily, uncovering not the usual hard scrabble of rocks but a loose accumulation of small rounded stones. Finn recognized the deposit immediately. His mother's brother Anton had made a comfortable fortune on a bed of high quality gravel out of a pit only ten miles from the Erikson farm. Finn evened the thin soil cover back over the gravel and dragged the dead steer to a new spot near the hayfield.

When Finn turned seventeen, Numi gave him the old rusted-out truck. Instead of driving it, Finn parked it in the back yard and proceeded to dismantle it. He went over to Polly Sirko's farm where he knew there was another truck, not quite as ancient as the one at home but in need of major repair. He convinced her to give him the vehicle in exchange for field work, of which he knew there was no possibility. Polly's sons had leased out the land for pasture when her husband died, and pretty much left her on her own and dependent on the goodwill of her neighbours. Poor old Polly was on the cusp of dementia and had long since lost track of the business affairs of her property. She was vulnerable to the charismatic young Finn with his beach-sand hair and cyan eyes, who sweet-talked her like a favourite grandson angling for cookies. Once he had the two trucks together, he matched parts and improvised connections and made changes until he had an operating version that was an improvement on both vehicles. Numi was impressed. Finn wanted a new box on the back of the truck and Numi helped to build it. Before long, and unknown to Numi, Finn was delivering small loads of gravel here and there and building his own bank account. He bought a small flatbed trailer and started collecting scrap metal and scouting junkyards for car parts, which he stored in the back end of the hayshed. Numi was unhappy about this, but he knew it was hopeless to try to stand up to the determined Finn.

Numi Erikson died of a heart attack when Finn was nineteen. He left everything to his favourite son. Gunnar and Karl did not attend the funeral or the reading of the will. No one knew where the sister Lynn was, and no effort was made to find her.

Finn never had any intention of operating a gravel pit. He found an appraiser to value the property, and put the land up for sale, except for the farmyard itself. New developments were moving into the areas north of the city, and the appetite for gravel for construction and roads was insatiable. The new owners of the gravel pit built an access to their property right off the highway. It was a perfect setup for Finn—a small farm in a depressed area of the Interlake, set on a dead-end road a mile back from the highway. Finn had all the buildings bulldozed, except the hayshed and the house. He installed running water in the house and fenced the yard site. He bought a used Mack truck and a heavy new flatbed so he could continue his rounds of auto junkyards. It wasn't long before he graduated to buying parts stripped from stolen vehicles. He closed in the old hayshed and used it to store his illegal inventory. Overnight, young Finn Erikson was a wealthy man.

But Finn still loved his big black Mack. He had the doors emblazoned with yellow and orange flames and overlaid the artwork with the words *Finn's Flying Transport*. He bought a forty-four foot livestock trailer and began contracting his services to Interlake ranchers and feedlots. He hated cattle—they were stupid animals—but the money was good in transporting them. Before long, Finn's Transport was moving loads back and forth from as far as Alberta. The long-distance hauls continued until he got caught at an inspection station with a load of calves on their way to a feedlot. Finn used to boast that he had a waitress at every truck stop, and he spent most of the night with one of them in Portage la Prairie while his truck was parked with the calves. When he finally got them on the road the next day, he was pulled into a weigh scale where the animals were found to be in grim condition. They were dehydrated and exhausted after more than twenty hours in the trailer. Some had collapsed and were injured; five were dead. Finn was forced to deliver his load immediately to the nearest cattle facility. He faced a significant fine for cruelty to animals and the owner of the calves refused to pay him for the incomplete trip. Furthermore, he had to reimburse the owner for the injured and lost livestock. Finn sold the cattle trailer and vowed he would never be trapped at an inspection station again.

Coincidence

I don't think that anything happens by coincidence...
No one is here by accident...

> *Everyone who crosses our path has a message for us.*
> *Otherwise they would have taken another path,*
> *or left earlier or later.*

The fact that these people are here
means that they are here for some reason...

> *We notice those chance events*
> *that occur at just the right moment,*
> *and bring forth just the right individuals,*
> *to suddenly send our lives in a new and important direction.*

James Redfield The Celestine Prophecy
Grand Central Publishing (1995)

chapter 7
Aunt Maggie's

Just west of the Manitoba-Ontario border, Finn eased his truck into the Department of Transport Weigh Station. Finn hated these stations but it wasn't worth it to take chances. He usually detoured around them but in this part of the country that was seldom possible. He wasn't particularly concerned; he knew his load was under the weight limits and his paperwork was in perfect order. Eight or ten trucks waited in line ahead of him. This was good. The busier the scales were, the more efficient the inspectors appeared to be, and the faster the vehicles cleared and were back on the highway. Finn had a friendly conversation with the scale operator, asking about road and traffic conditions. They discussed the dark cloud of weather rolling in on a cold front. The operator glanced at Finn's perfectly correct truckers log and sent him on his way.

The rain started just as Finn was gearing down for the Kenora exit. Driven into sharp little spits by the strengthening wind, it spattered thinly on his windshield. Only slightly annoying, it didn't quite warrant the wipers. Finn down-ramped onto the exit and pulled his truck into the wide parking lot of Aunt Maggie's Truck Stop just as the cloud unleashed its cold deluge.

Finn dripped into Aunt Maggie's and made his way to his customary spot in the last corner booth by the window. It was right beside the kitchen and most diners preferred not to be close to the clatter and chatter of the staff, but Finn didn't mind. From this vantage point he could see almost all of the parking lot and virtually everyone in the restaurant. This always made him smile. He liked to watch people. Finn felt like a Wild West outlaw with his back to the wall, ready for whomever might come in the door.

He smelled Erica before he saw her. A thick shadow of flowers and musk followed her from the kitchen to the coffee station and on to her section of tables. There had been some complaints about the overpowering fragrance but Erica saw it as one of her personal rights. And she was after all the manager of Maggie's and who was going to do anything about it?

Erica knew all the truckers well. She leaned over Finn from behind, her breast brushing against his shoulder, to pour coffee into an oversized mug. She slid the dish of creamers close to it. Finn inhaled her flowery scent.

"Lunch, Finn?" Erica toyed with her order pad and tried to be nonchalant.

Finn was already late and had not planned on eating—this would just be a coffee break—but the restaurant was redolent with smells of meat and gravy and some kind of spicy dessert. The rain slapped against the window and he could hear the east wind mobilizing itself to storm strength. He decided to stay for lunch. A good meal might help the headache.

"Couple of Advil to start with. And I'll have the special. What is it, anyway?"

"Hot beef sandwich with fries and coleslaw. Or you can have veggies instead of the slaw. And pie is included."

Finn yawned. "Slaw, kiddo. And a side of onion rings. And cherry pie if you have it."

"Sure thing. I'll be back right away with your Advil."

Erica disappeared into the racket of the kitchen. Finn could still smell her perfume dancing with the aroma of roast beef.

Along the wall across from Finn and two tables down, a young couple waited for their lunch. The woman faced Finn and a small dark-haired girl was sandwiched in beside her, next to the wall. Specks of blue glitter sparkled on the girl's forehead and cheeks. Finn could tell by the red blotchiness of her face that she had been crying. The child toyed listlessly with the crayons and paper activity placemat in front of her, tearing little strips from the mat and piling them by her plate. She pulled a red plastic wallet from the butterfly pocket on the front of her t-shirt and stuffed a couple of strips into it. She looked up and directly at Finn, returning his stare. Finn didn't ordinarily pay any attention to children; he didn't like them at all. He didn't like this child either, but there was something compelling about her. Intuition was not common to Finn and his brain was clumsy as he tried to classify his reaction to the girl. All he could see were her eyes, rimmed with red sadness and impossibly dark and too large for her face. The eyes reminded him inexplicably of an incident with a black kitten when he was a young boy. The kitten was his mother's pet and he had accidentally backed over it with their old truck, right in front of her, not quite killing it. His father Numi was there too, and forced eleven-year-old Finn to dispatch the poor animal immediately with a shovel while his mother watched. Every once in a while something caused the event to resurface. There would be the pleading terrified eyes of the kitten, his mother's muffled sobs (as much for Finn as for the animal), and his father turning his back on both of them and kicking an old pail across the yard into the barbed wire fence.

"Here's your Advil."

Finn snapped back to the child's beseeching stare and the eyes of the kitten faded backward into his mind like a dream folding in on itself at first wakefulness. It was unsettling. Finn was not given to perception, but this family bothered him and he couldn't quite decide why.

Erica set a glass of ice water in front of him. "Your special will be out in a minute, Finn. Can I get you anything else?"

He stared at the outline of her breasts and grinned. "Let me think about that for a minute."

"I was here early this morning, Finn. I wish you would've called to let me know you weren't coming."

"Sorry. I got sidetracked by a bash last night. Maybe I'll catch you on the way back."

"When's that going to be?"

"Early tomorrow morning, I hope."

"So, where you headed this trip?"

"Drop off at Thunder Bay, load to pick up at Nipigon."

"And you're talking about being back here tomorrow morning? Finn, why the hell do you do that?"

"Do what?"

"Why do you push these long trips when you don't have to?"

"I like to break my own records, I guess."

"I don't get it. Anyway, I'd like to see how you're going to record a trip like that in your log."

"When I get back maybe I'll let you record my log."

"Finn, you're an impossible jerk." She grinned in spite of herself and returned to the heat rack to pick up an order.

MARGARET RIDDELL

The door of the restaurant opened and a wet gust swept into the room. Two cyclists, soaked and dripping, made their way to the booth next to Finn's and directly across from the couple with the child. They peeled off their wet jackets and hung them on the coat hooks at the end of the booth. Erica appeared promptly with two menus.

"Can I get you two something to drink before you order?"

They both stared at the red Formica table top as if it had the answer.

"Just ice water for me," the young man said. "With a thick slice of lemon."

"I'll have a chocolate milkshake," the woman said. There was an edge to her voice, as if she dared her partner to comment. He did not.

"Okay, I'll be right back to take your order."

Finn had seen the couple pull up to the restaurant on their matching bikes. They parked the dark green Cannondales close to the windows where they would be within sight and under the eaves of the building out of the rain. A little late to worry about the weather, Finn observed.

Finn had nothing but contempt for cyclists. There was no gray area to his position. He hated them in the city, where he believed they enjoyed special undeserved privileges, and he hated them on the highway where he believed they endangered themselves and everyone else every time they pulled out on to the pavement. Road lice, he called them.

Finn sat back in his booth and enjoyed their wet unhappiness. From fragments of the tense whispered conversation he could tell something had gone awry. The cyclists intended cross-country tour would be cut short in Winnipeg. From there, the young woman planned to take the bus back to Halifax, with her bike in the underbus cargo hold. From what Finn could make out of their subdued conversation, it sounded like the man would continue on to his brother's place in Brandon. One more night on the road together. Then, maybe they would see each other again sometime. Maybe during the fall semester at Dalhousie.

And maybe not, thought Finn. He smirked.

Food finally arrived at the young family's table—minestrone soup and chicken salad sandwiches for the man and woman, chicken nuggets and red jelly for the girl. Kelly, the other waitress at Aunt Maggie's Restaurant, fussed to get everything arranged on the small table.

The man pointed to the placemat and crayons.

"You need to put that stuff away and make room for your food."

The girl gathered the torn paper strips and stuffed them in a pocket on the front of her blue t-shirt, along with the red plastic wallet. There was a whispered argument, something about someone called Emily. Evidently the child hated Emily.

"But I need to go to the restroom."

The woman shook her head. "Wait till we're finished and I'll take you."

The child sobbed audibly. "I really, really, really need to pee."

"Let her go," the man said. "It's just around the corner. She can't get lost."

Reluctantly, the woman slid out of her seat to let the child out.

From his privileged vantage point Finn could still see the girl around the corner. She pulled a torn scrap of placemat and what looked to Finn like a piece of broken crayon from the kangaroo pocket on the front of her T-shirt. She squinted out the doorway towards the parking lot. She smoothed the bit of paper on a narrow shelf on the wall outside the restroom and toiled away with the crayon. Finn doubted she would be old enough to actually write anything. She lifted a flap inside the red wallet and placed the strip of paper underneath it. She stood leaning against the wall as if trying to decide what to do next. She was still crying.

Uncharacteristically, Finn contemplated going to the child. With an almost involuntary motion he pushed his chair back from the table a little. Without knowing what he would do or say, he began to stand.

At that moment a tall elderly man came out of the restroom. His sandy-coloured comb-over fluttered in a wild flyaway over his head. He looked from side to side, bewildered, as if trying to decide where to go, and then approached the child Finn had been watching. There was an animated whispered conversation between the two. The man bent and pulled the child close and hugged her.

They must know each other, Finn decided. He sat back down in his chair. The urge to intervene passed. He settled back in his seat and looked over his shoulder towards the kitchen to see if there was any sign of his lunch.

The child was still crying and the tall man pulled a crinkled tissue from the pocket of his pilly navy sweater and wiped the sad little face. The child handed something to him. Someone called, "Are you coming, Dad?" The man frowned and looked around as if he couldn't for the life of him imagine who the voice might belong to. He leaned closer to the child and whispered something to her and pointed toward a telephone booth.

A tall blond man, the owner of the voice, came forward and took the old man's arm and gently led him outside.

The girl went directly to an old pay phone just outside the restrooms and stretched to reach the receiver. Little fingers poked at the numbers. Yeah, right, whispered Finn under his breath. He doubted she would have had any idea how to use the payphone. There was no way of telling whether she reached anyone on the other end. If she did, the conversation was very short.

Outside, Finn could see the elderly man being shepherded towards a grey Buick. He was holding his hands over his head in a futile effort to keep the rain from falling on his sparse hair. The younger man deposited his father in the front passenger seat, settled himself behind the wheel, and they drove off into the rain.

The child returned to her chair. She put her head down and refused to look at her parents. Only two or three minutes had passed since she left the table.

"Now eat your lunch," the woman said. "And hurry up. We have to go." She looked around the restaurant and whispered something to the man. He knotted his brows and nodded his head.

Erica set Finn's hot beef sandwich platter in front of him and slid into the opposite side of the booth. "Okay if I take a coffee break with you? Kelly'll bring your pie around."

"Sure, kiddo." He winked. "Seeing as how I didn't get to see you this morning."

Erica slipped off her shoes and worked her toes under his pant leg along the side of his ankle. Finn slathered ketchup on his fries and dumped the little paper container of coleslaw on his plate beside the sandwich. He nodded towards the table across the aisle.

"What's with them?"

Erica shrugged. "Something about the kid wanting to go home. I tried to joke with her, you know, to take her mind off it? But the kid just ignored me and the parents didn't even look up. Weird family."

"Takes all kinds, as they say." Finn leaned his chair back. "Not our problem." He floated the remaining fries in more ketchup.

The family pushed back from the table.

"I don't want you to complain about being hungry," the man said. "It's going to be a long time before we can stop again."

They moved to the cash register by the door, arguing inaudibly about something. The woman brushed a few stray hairs back from the child's forehead. Kelly made change for the twenty the man handed her, and gave the little girl a green-striped peppermint.

The couple hurried through the rain to their vehicle which was parked right outside the window where Finn and Erica sat. The child was firmly in hand between the two adults, but she was resisting, pulling back, trying to twist away. A small tussle ensued. She dropped something and stretched back, reaching for it on the ground, but the woman turned back and kicked a flash of something red toward the gas pumps. They placed the now-howling child in the back seat of a red station wagon and buckled her into a booster seat.

As the station wagon backed away from the window, Erica stared in disbelief. The licence plate on the car was ELS111. That in itself wasn't extraordinary to anyone but Erica. It jumped out at her, because it was exactly the same as the password she used for her email. It consisted of her initials, ELS, standing for Erica Lynn Slesiuk, and one-one-one, representing her birthdate, January 11th. She gaped at the improbability of this.

The station wagon spun from the parking lot. Finn could see the child lurch forward when the brakes engaged at the stop sign before the access. The car accelerated onto the highway, spewing wet gravel behind.

Erica told Finn about the license plate but he just laughed.

"You read too much into things, Erica."

Kelly arrived with Finn's cherry pie. "Is there anything else I can get for you?"

Finn nodded at the coffeepot. "How 'bout a refill?"

Erica's toes continued to work on his ankles. Kelly filled their cups and moved on to the table where the couple and child had been sitting. Finn watched the motion of her firm rear end as she gathered the dishes and wiped the table. He stored the information for future reference.

Kelly set the lemon water and chocolate milkshake in front of the cyclists and stood with her order pad. They finally decided on the clubhouse special. No fries, could they get a salad instead? Kelly scribbled the order as she turned toward the kitchen. Finn watched her shapely behind as she walked away. She looked back over her shoulder at Erica, who worked her toes a little higher on Finn's ankle.

"You finished your break yet?" Kelly gestured toward the kitchen. "Could use some help here."

Finn placed a couple of toonies beside the empty coffee mug for Erica. He pushed back from the table and his chair grated on the dried mud where his feet had been. Kelly met him at the cash register. He had a tip for her, too. He picked up an Auto Trader and a Winnipeg Free Press on his way out. It was three o'clock.

chapter 8

Booker's Last Trip

Booker Johnson had not quite reached the stage where he had to be accompanied to the restroom. He was still fully cognisant of knowing when he needed to go, and was able to manipulate the restroom stall doors and toilet paper and hot-air hand dryers. In all likelihood he had no idea where on the map he was, but he was happy just to be on the road. Someone usually hovered around the door of the restroom in case Booker got his directions turned around when he came out, but for the most part he managed with no problems.

Booker finished with the toilet and flushed it. He rinsed his hands under the cold water tap and thrust them under the rust-spotted air dryer. It wasn't working well, and he ended up wiping his hands on his pilly navy cardigan on the way out the door. He had recently developed the habit of looking at the floor when he walked, as if he was eternally searching for something, so he didn't notice the girl until he bumped into her.

The child was crying. Booker patted her on the head in a grandfatherly gesture.

"What's the matter, sweetie?"

"I'm Nellie, and I need help."

Booker leaned to put his arm around the little shoulder. He put a finger under the child's chin and tipped her face upward. "Tell Grampy what's wrong."

"My name is Nellie," the girl whispered. "Some bad people took me away from my mommy."

Booker's altruistic instincts lurched into overdrive. "Where are the bad people?"

The child pointed in the direction of the restaurant. She pulled away from Booker and dug a scrap of paper from the pocket in the front of her blue t-shirt. "Here," she said. "This is the name of their car."

The thick crayon printing was indecipherable to Booker in the dim light of the hallway. Even in good light he would probably not have been able to make sense of the letters. He squinted at the scrap of paper in his hand and moved it back and forth, trying to find a distance where he could focus. It made sense and it didn't make sense. He scrunched the scrap in the palm of his hand and tried to bring his mind to bear on the puzzle.

A tall young man leaned on the checkout counter of the restaurant. He had sandy blond hair and brown eyes like Booker's. The relationship was obvious.

"All done, Dad? Ready to go?" He held up a large bag of Scotch mints. "Got your favourite treat for you."

Booker's eyes darted back and forth between the child and the man at the counter, who was his son Randy. Booker had just time to lean down to the child and whisper something in her ear before Randy gently took his elbow and herded him toward the exit.

Their car was parked directly outside the door.

"Is this a new car?" Booker asked Randy.

"No, Dad. It's the same old one."

There was some confusion on Booker's part as to whether he should be driving or getting into the passenger seat. That was quickly resolved, and they exited gently onto the highway, headed west. Booker's wife Bonnie relaxed in the back seat.

Booker strained to look back at the restaurant. "Nellie needs me to help her," he said, with determined urgency.

"Who?" asked Randy. "Who's Nellie?"

"That little girl back there. She was crying."

Bonnie reached her hand over the back of the seat and patted her husband on the shoulder.

"It's all right, honey. She'll be fine."

Booker became increasingly agitated.

"No, no. She needs me to help." He unfolded his fist and brandished the crumpled paper. "Nellie gave me the name."

Randy and Bonnie exchanged knowing glances. Bonnie made a mental note that Booker's delusions and confusions were definitely becoming worse and more frequent. No one paid any attention to the wrinkled paper and Booker folded it into a little square and put it in his pocket.

"Where are we going?"

"We're headed home, Dad. Back to Winnipeg."

Booker was visibly puzzled.

"Back to Winnipeg?"

No one responded. Everyone had lost track of the number of times the question had been asked in the past three weeks. Headed east, the answer had been Niagara Falls. Just as Booker seemed to begin to understand a particular destination, it was reached, visited, and in the past. On the return trip the answer had changed from Niagara Falls to Winnipeg, and Booker was increasingly bewildered.

"Is this a new car?" he asked again.

"No, Dad. Same old car."

Randy had taken Booker and Bonnie on what would be their last vacation. They wanted to make the trip while Booker might still get some enjoyment out of the journey. Arrangements were in place for Booker to check in at the Belle Vista Lodge personal care home when they returned to Winnipeg.

Bonnie painstakingly planned the trip to mirror, as nearly as possible, their honeymoon to Niagara Falls nearly fifty years ago. They had done much exotic travel over the years since then, but oddly had never returned to Niagara. Bonnie always wanted to go back, so the trip was as much for her as for Booker. But it was anything but relaxing.

Booker enjoyed the drive through the rolling Ontario farm-lands and was fascinated by the ride on the Chi-Cheemaun Ferry from Tobermory, although most of his delight centred not upon the scenery but upon the hundreds of seagulls that fol-lowed the passage. At Niagara, however, he did seem to appreci-ate the falls and the ride on the Maid-O-The-Mist.

Booker wanted to swim in Lake Superior when they stopped along its shores on the way home and pouted when he had to return to the car. And when they visited Ouimet Canyon, Randy had to restrain him from squeezing around the barriers when he wanted to teeter on the edge of the steep cliff.

Each place they visited, no matter how breathtaking, was rel-egated to non-memory. Every day was new, but Booker remem-bered only the immediate past. Every time they got into the car to resume their journey, Booker started with a clean slate.

And now they had reached the last day of the trip. They had travelled well together, notwithstanding the stresses of contend-ing with Booker.

Despite Booker's rapidly progressing dementia it was not unusual for him to obsessively latch on to something. Now, he clutched at the wrinkled scrap of paper. *I have to find somewhere safe to hide it. Somewhere safe.*

"There was a little girl," Booker insisted. He looked over his shoulder, past Bonnie in the back seat, and strained to see out the rear window. "She gave me the name."

Randy was used to cryptic comments like this from Booker. He reached into the console.

"How about some music, Dad? What would you like to listen to"?

"Do we have some bagpipe music tapes?" Booker still called them tapes, although it was years since Randy had owned anything besides CD's.

They did indeed have bagpipe "tapes." As of late, it was Booker's music of choice. They had listened to it many times over the past two weeks. The CD was titled *Scotland the Brave* and was a compilation of twenty-one selections—enough shrill wailing to last over an hour. Bonnie shuddered involuntarily. Randy sighed. *I guess we can tolerate it one last time*, he thought. He slid the disk into the slot and the pipes launched into the plaintive skirl of the Skye Boat Song. Pacified, Booker relaxed. The same couldn't be said for Randy and Bonnie.

Booker leaned his head back on the headrest and closed his eyes.

"We have to help the little girl," he whispered. "Bad people, bad people."

The bagpipe music filled the small space of the car. Booker looked over at Randy, trying to decipher their relationship. He frowned as if trying to compute something in his head.

"Is this a new car?" he asked.

chapter 9
The Highwayman

Restaurant parking lots are productive. People leave their cars, enter the restaurant, and stay inside for as long as it takes to have a meal. Sometimes they leave their vehicles within sight of the windows, but just as often they park them further away from the building or around at the side where they can be in the shade, perhaps, or out of the wind. About seventy-five percent of the time they lock the cars. Jervis Oswald Strunk specialized in the twenty-five percent that were left unlocked.

Restaurant patrons took an average of fifty minutes for lunch, from one and a half to two hours for dinner, and half an hour or less for breakfast, based on Jervis's surveillance over the years. Buffets and fast-foods and truck stops took less time. It depended on the type of restaurant, of course, and whether the diner was alone or with friends or family. People lingered longer when the weather was inclement and tended to hurry their meals when the establishment was crowded.

However, if there was one thing Jervis Strunk had learned over the years it was that none of his observations guaranteed complete predictability. He had experienced a few close calls when people came out too soon, and those had taught him to operate more efficiently.

Just before noon Jervis pulled his old grey Ford Fairmont up close to the west side of the truck stop where there was some shelter from the driving rain. He slouched as low down as he could get into the front seat. The slit between the top of the steering wheel and the dash was just wide enough for him to peer out without being noticed. A sporty yellow convertible, top up against the rain, eased into the parking space beside him. Jervis compacted himself even further and pretended to sleep. He was barely noticeable through the drops of rain on the window. He watched as two young men dressed in suits climbed out of the convertible and hurried into the restaurant. He waited five minutes before stepping out into the rain himself. He opened the unlocked door of the convertible and popped open the glove compartment. With a practiced hand he swept inside. It was like a mystery grab bag, he always thought, you never knew what you might come up with. This time there was a fat tan leather organizer wallet (a woman's, from the look of it), a Canon mini-camera, and a red pocket flashlight. Without missing a beat, he slid back into the Ford and inspected his plunder. The wallet held at least a dozen credit cards and over a hundred dollars cash. He slipped the items into the glove compartment, locked the door, and followed the men into the diner. Less than two minutes had passed.

Jervis found a vacant table right inside the door and slid into a chair next to the window. He pretended to study the menu while he allowed himself to relax. He had some projects planned for later in the day, and was counting on the weather to improve.

In the summer, Jervis Strunk was a creature of the highway. He lived in his car. He parked overnight mostly in lots at big-box malls or at Walmart. Occasionally he used highway rest stops. He kept to himself and never stayed in a spot more than one night. He kept the car clean and in good repair. The vehicle attracted little attention.

Jervis's main place of business was the Trans-Canada Highway between Brandon and Thunder Bay. In a good season, between the parked cars and the shopping centres and the shady deals, he could rip off enough goods and money to see him through the winter. He always returned to Winnipeg in early November. He paid a slum landlord a hundred dollars to park the Ford on a derelict lot in north Winnipeg behind a junkyard and he moved into the Main Street shelter. Although he got along well with the staff, by the end of April he was always sick and tired of the rules. The ten o'clock curfew annoyed him the most, almost as much as having to sign in and out of the place. Drinking and smoking and drug use was not allowed, but that was of no concern to him; he didn't indulge in these anyway. Fighting with other residents was also forbidden, but he managed to keep to himself and made little contact with anyone. With the arrival of spring, Jervis would retrieve his car and be on the road again.

Jervis's seat at the table faced the two men from the yellow sports car. They ordered Denver sandwiches and fries and Pepsi, and Jervis made a mental note of how long their order might take. He ordered black coffee and a toasted cinnamon bun for himself. When the bun arrived he broke it into small pieces. The Denver sandwiches had not shown up yet.

Jervis could feel that he was being watched. A very small girl stared at him intently from a few tables away. Jervis had a soft spot for little girls, especially little girls with long dark hair. He stared back at the child. He was sure he had seen her somewhere recently—so very recently, in fact, that it felt like deja-vue. But where? He realized he was returning her stare and he looked away. He finished the sections of cinnamon bun and picked at the crumbs on his plate.

The waitress set the Denver sandwiches on the table in front of the two young men. Jervis quickly finished his coffee and scraped his chair back from the table. It was important to leave first.

chapter 10
The Cyclists

The cyclists first met in the parking lot of the Grawood campus pub at Dalhousie University in Halifax. Well, they weren't actually cyclists yet; that was to come later. It was a Wednesday Wing Night. John Lindblom had come to watch a hockey game on the wide-screen television, and Katie Maybank, as usual, was there to play Sex Toy Bingo with three of her girlfriends.

Katie won twice—a multi-colour glow-in-the-dark vibrator and a kit of assorted fruit-flavoured body paints. Her companions insisted on a little extra celebrating (she was the only winner in their group) and by the time they left the bar at midnight none of them were in any condition to drive. A Yellow Cab was on its way.

Katie tripped on a bump the size of a cookie and as she put her arms out to break her fall the vibrator spun across the parking lot, followed by the body paint. The girlfriends laughed uproariously. Katie contemplated the pavement close to her face and pushed herself up to a sitting position. A wide scrape stung her knee. She felt something touch her shoulder and turned to see the silhouette of a man with his hand extended towards her.

"Need a hand getting up?" The three girlfriends giggled loudly at the obviousness of the question. Katie latched on to the proffered assistance and noticed her vibrator and the kit of body paint in the man's other hand. The spin across the parking lot had somehow activated the switch and the vibrator was humming and changing colour from green to blue to red.

John examined the prizes. "Where do you live? I'll drive you home."

She nodded. The girlfriends were hysterical.

"By the way, I'm John. We'll have to walk back to the residence to pick up my car. Can you make it?"

She giggled and allowed him to prop her up under his arm and they wavered down the sidewalk in the direction of the residence hall.

The cross-Canada bike trip had been poorly conceived from the beginning. Neither of the students had any experience with long distance rides. Their physical conditioning was sketchy at best, and they had been unable to settle on an itinerary. They consistently dismissed any advice that might have been helpful. They never had a chance.

The cramped confines of the tiny tent had been most opportune at the beginning of the cross-country adventure when they believed they were crazily in love, but by the time John and Katie reached northwestern Ontario the early romantic days of the relationship were cold history. Nights in the tent were tense and edgy. The strain of being together twenty-four hours, days on end, had exacted its toll. They were seeing each other in the light of familiarity, and it had turned out to be less than flattering.

chapter 11
Tour's End

Katie Maybank's Cannondale was in need of repairs and an attendant at a garage gave her companion John Lindblom the address of a cycle shop in Keewatin where they could get quick service. John had done his best with maintenance along the way but Katie never did seem to grasp the importance of this. She relied upon John to check and service her bicycle when he did his own. The helplessness he found so endearing at first now irritated and frustrated him.

Checking and tightening nuts and bolts, lubricating (she didn't even know the difference between grease and oil), examining the chains and cables, the brake and derailleur levers—it was a lengthy checklist and he refused to deviate from it. But he was out of patience. He was tired of doing all the work while she fussed with her appearance and packed and repacked her clothing, half of which had to be crammed into one of his panniers because she had insisted on bringing so many things.

They shivered under their rain gear in a grungy little park across the road from the Keewatin Cycle Shop while the repairs were completed. The service was not as fast as had been promised. Katie paid for the work with her credit card and they wheeled out onto the road and from there entered the highway. Both bikes were Cannondales, dark green. John had owned his since his first year at Dalhousie, and Katie found one second hand at Cyclesmith on Quinpool Road in Halifax, just after they germinated the idea of crossing the country.

Three kilometers down the road they exited to a truck stop and chained the bikes together close to the building. It was still pouring and they were cold and drenched in spite of the rain gear. They entered the restaurant on a gust of wind and made their way to a newly-cleared booth by the window, from where there was a full view of the bikes. They hung their dripping jackets on coat hooks at the end of the booth.

Most of the restaurant patrons were able to grab the gist of the tense, almost whispered conversation between the pair. *The intended cross-country tour would be cut short. It was a final decision. Too bad it turned out to be such a fiasco, the man said. Something had gone badly awry, but they would continue on, once the rain stopped, for as long as it took to get to Winnipeg. They both had people to visit there, it seemed. From there the young woman would take the bus back to Halifax with her bike in the underbus cargo hold. The man would continue on to see his brother in Brandon. A couple more nights on the road, the woman said, but there was no sadness in the statement, just a palpable sense of relief. Then maybe they would see each other again back at classes in the fall, she said. He nodded absently, and it was obvious that the comment was empty, meaningless.*

A young family sat at the table directly across from John and Katie. A child, a little girl of four or five, was blubbering into a sodden tissue. The mother whispered something into her ear.

"No, I don't want Emily," the girl said. "I hate Emily."

The man and woman whispered and gestured between themselves. The mother made another attempt at conversation.

MARGARET RIDDELL

A small tantrum ensued and the child threw something onto the floor. "I hate Emily! And I really really really need to pee."

"All right then, I'll take you. Just a minute," the mother said.

"No, I don't want you to come. I can go by myself."

"Let her go", the man said. "She can't get lost. It's just around the corner."

Katie leaned out from her chair, trying to get a closer look at the girl as she passed their table. "I think something is wrong there, John," she said. "I just have a feeling."

"It's just your overactive imagination." He picked a piece of wilted lettuce from his turkey club sandwich. "Besides, it's none of our business."

Outside, the rain continued. They decided to set up camp for the night rather than continue the westward ride, although it was still early afternoon. The weather was supposed to improve overnight; they would get an early start in the morning.

On the Road

There is a population of many millions
on our roads and highways at any given time.
It's like a massive cross-country city on the move.
Everyone is anonymous.
There are no provincial or state boundaries in effect out there,
and there is no limit to criminal opportunity.
As long as there have been established routes for travel,
there have been opportunistic criminals lying in wait
to take advantage of travelers.
The story of the Good Samaritan
relates the attack by thieves upon a man travelling
from Jerusalem to Jericho in Biblical times.
In the Middle Ages, bandits and highwaymen
flourished on the roads of Europe,
and wayfarers banded together for safety in travelling.
In the early days of settlement in North America,
outlaws made their living from holdups
of stagecoaches, trains, and mail deliveries.
Modern highway crime has evolved
to include vehicle hijacking and robberies of personal vehicles,
freeway snipers and rapists, serial killers and road rage.
No place is truly safe.

chapter 12
The King's Highway

The windshield wipers slapped back and forth at high speed. Every so often a violent gust shuddered the blades and threatened to tear them from the wiper arms. The wind ate up Finn's mileage efficiency but he would probably still make it to Nipigon before midnight. It was a six hour drive from Kenora to Thunder Bay, so just after six he pulled into a rest stop near Ignace, parked at the far end of the lot and entered his sleeper. Finn's deluxe custom cab was state of the art. He used the large double bed often—for sleeping, when he chose to, but just as often for entertaining guests. He had a prototype incinerating toilet installed in the sleeper, and fondly referred to it as his "turd burner." The toilet was a sleek gas-fuelled apparatus capable of reducing one "sittings" waste to a tablespoon of fine, odorless ash. Finn put the requisite liner in the bowl of the toilet and did his business. When he finished he flipped a switch and washed his hands at his stainless steel sink while he waited for the incineration cycle to complete. Women usually expressed aversion to the toilet at first but it was generally a hit once they realized how well it worked. Finn took three Red Bulls from his refrigerator, along with two Eatmore bars, and returned to the driver's seat.

It was still windy and raining. On the highway, reflections of approaching daytime lights quavered on the wet pavement. Finn popped two extra strength Advils with his Red Bull and finished off an Eatmore before lighting up an Export A. A small car blew past him near the end of an uphill passing lane and the driver took his time moving over so that Finn had to brake. Finn accelerated and deliberately tailgated the car for more than ten minutes before backing off.

A murky layer of low cloud bullied away any summer daylight that would have lingered past nine o'clock on one of the longest days of summer. Finn imagined he could see a faint pink slit in the western sky far behind him, but in front of him everything was as black as a power failure. Finn opened another Red Bull. Across the median to his left, the Terry Fox Monument slid past like a pained ghost above the wet blue lights of its base. Finn held the Red Bull can up in a crooked salute. He admired guts.

Finn rolled into the truckers' parking area at Granny's Trucker Haven at nine-fifteen, in time for a late dinner before continuing east. Aunt Maggie's, Granny's—Finn never really gave it much thought, but he was drawn to restaurants with "comfort" names. Granny's was well off the Trans-Canada close to a string of hotels, but it was well worth the sidetrack. The dark paneled walls and tinted windows afforded privacy for those who wanted it—customers could either sit at a long lunch bar with blue vinyl seats or at booths along the windows. Finn always chose the booth furthest from the door if it was available. Izzie was the waitress of note at Thunder Bay, and Finn was disappointed she wasn't working the late shift. He would have had time. The woman who appeared at his table was thin

MARGARET RIDDELL

and tired-looking. Unlike Izzie, who could take a full order and never had to write a single word and never made a mistake, this waitress recorded Finn's order laboriously on her pad: thick ribeye steak, rare, baked potato with the works, scratch the broccoli, a side of onion rings. Finn squinted at the waitress' straggly blonde hair and broken fingernails. Even with her painstaking documentation of his order, he didn't trust her to get things right.

"I want that steak still jumpin'!" he said in a voice loud enough to startle her. "Make sure you tell the cook."

The woman nodded nervously and retreated with his order like a frightened pup. Through the heat rack opening Finn could hear her speaking urgently to someone in the kitchen.

Finn set his trucker's log on the table and smoothed it open. He recorded the dates of this particular trip as July 1 and 2 and printed his name in block lettering. There was no employee number to worry about; in this space he overwrote the squares with "Self Employed." He had load numbers for the pickup address in Thunder Bay, just in case. He checked his Daily Vehicle Inspection Report (this was always 100% true) which was duly signed off on by his friendly personal mechanic and sometime business partner before he left Winnipeg.

The part of the log Finn most enjoyed was the challenge of the graph grid. Here he got to document his circumvention of any regulations he didn't agree with. He always thought the finished graph looked like a city skyline—a skyline he got to build however he saw fit. For this trip, he recorded the starting time as eight o'clock on the morning of July 1, although he had really left at eleven on the second. Using the edge of a credit card to keep his lines perfectly straight, Finn made little gutters in his landscape to mark on-duty time for fuelling up or stopping to get loaded. Uninterrupted driving cut a line through the fifteen minutes markings of the grid and Finn made a point of keeping these lines no longer than five hours. Stopping for meals made the line form little skyscrapers, always the same height and usually an hour wide. When the trucking day was hypothetically over, the thin black line moved to the "Sleeper" row on the graph. Finn usually recorded these segments as anywhere from seven to nine hours; this night, he decided on eight. Beneath the graph, angled comments parsed the skyline. Lunch, Kenora. Rest Stop, English River, Thunder Bay, supper. Thunder Bay, loading.

The log was perfect, so far as he could tell. In his opinion, it was no one's business where and for how long he drove, slept, and ate. It gave him great satisfaction to circumvent the system.

Finn opened the newspapers he picked up in Kenora. The Auto Trader was always interesting, but Finn wasn't in the market for anything right then. He just liked to keep abreast of what was out there. The Winnipeg Free Press, however, caused him to do a double take. The large picture on the front page was unmistakably that of the little girl he saw at Maggie's Truck Stop. *Without a Trace*, blared the headline. Under the photo were the words, *Have You Seen This Child?*

Finn's supper arrived, delivered by the nervous waitress and a helper from the kitchen. He sliced into the huge ribeye and was pleased to see the red meat leaking its juice onto his plate. The waitress refilled his coffee and crept back to the kitchen. Finn was hungry. He stuffed a piece of steak the size of a deck of cards into his mouth and leaned back in his seat. Relaxed, he took in the ambience of the restaurant with its honey-coloured log walls and oiled wood-plank floors. Granny's Trucker Haven lived up to its name.

What the crap? Finn sat upright. *It can't be.*

But it was. The same couple he and Erica had seen at Aunt Maggie's Truck Stop in Kenora was seated on the other side of the restaurant, partly hidden by a divider of artificial ferns and dusty pink chrysanthemums. They had just finished their meal, Finn guessed, because the man was waving to a waiter for their bill. The child, the girl of the photograph in the newspaper, leaned against the woman's shoulder, struggling to keep her dark kitten-eyes open. The man gathered the near-sleeping child in his arms and carried her out to their car while the woman went to the counter to pay for their meal. They passed close to Finn. If they recognized him from earlier in the day, they gave no sign. He could make out blotchy streaks on the child's face where tears had broken trails through traces of something blue on her cheeks.

Finn's earlier impulse to intervene had evaporated. He decided he would phone in an anonymous tip as soon as he got back to Winnipeg. He had no desire to involve himself with the police on this particular trip.

chapter 13
Mike And Erica

Mike Slesiuk dipped his hands into the tub of industrial-strength hand cleaner and worked the thick white gel over his palms and between his fingers. Left hand first, always. He spread a layer of cool gel across the palm of his hand, moving from pinky to thumb and then back again for good measure. Right hand, exact same routine. He removed the blackened sludge with a shop rag and repeated the process. Twice, three more times, a fresh rag each time, until finally the gel wiped off clear. He smelled his hands—citrus with a hint of petroleum—clean like a freshly-waxed car.

He gathered the dirty shop rags and piled them in a 45-gallon drum for RagTag Exchange to pick up. Mike's supply of clean shop rags was dwindling. He probably used more shop rags than anyone else on RagTag's client list. He made a mental note to call them first thing in the morning to order a new supply. He removed his dark green shop coveralls and folded them into a neat square before placing them on top of the shop rags.

He pushed the drum back into its place beside the door, gathered his backpack (after emptying it of the remains of his lunch), pulled the heavy door down and exited by the smaller door of Slesiuk Auto Repair. He turned the key in the lock, turned the knob three times to make sure it was engaged, and proceeded to his truck. He decided to return to the door to check the deadbolt again, just to be sure, and executed one last twist and pull on the knob. Everything appeared to be secure.

He pulled onto the access road and stopped at the stop sign and counted his full three seconds before easing on to the highway. Thirty kilometers an hour until the second power pole, then up to forty by the next pole, and after that it was all right to get up to speed, but never over the limit.

It was a ten-minute drive to the truck stop. Erica would be waiting, and she would be angry and impatient if Mike was late. He hated to make Erica angry, because she managed to turn every situation into a no-holds-barred battle. In the beginning her fiery disposition was one of the things he loved about her, but their relationship was exhausting. He was tired.

Erica was ready to go home. It had been a long day. She looked out the window to see if Mike had arrived but his truck was not there, so to put in time she helped Kelly clean the last of the tables and checked once again to make sure everything was in order. Lynne and Marty had already arrived and were having a smoke in the staff room before their shift. There was a tangle of menus beside the cash register and Erica stopped to sort them on her way out the door. She straightened what was left of the little local weekly, the *Northern Shield*, and the half-dozen copies of the *Winnipeg Free Press*. The Free Press was delivered daily to many centres in the Kenora area; many of the residents felt more like Manitobans than Ontarians anyway.

Erica smoothed the top copy of the newspaper. Under her hand was a picture of a small girl holding a teddy bear. The headline jumped out at Erica. *Have You Seen this Child?* She recognized the child at once—she was the one who had sat at the table across from Finn—the sad little girl with the remains of blue sparkles on her face. Erica folded the newspaper and tucked it under her arm. She would call the police on her cell phone the minute she got into the truck. She checked outside once more. Still no Mike. She went into the staff room and lit up a cigarette and dialed his cell number. No answer.

Erica was not waiting outside when Mike turned in to Maggie's. He pulled up under the overhead canopy beside one of the gas pumps and got out to clean the windshield, even though it was still raining. He preferred to do chores like that before Erica got into the truck, because for some reason not clear to Mike the procedure always irked her. He followed his routine: start on the driver's side windshield; pull the squeegee in wide loops, always from the top. Give the squeegee two shakes. Wipe the rubber blade with a carefully folded paper towel after each pass. Then to the rear view mirror and driver's side window, and on around the vehicle, always ending with the passenger side. A fresh dip into the water bucket and a clean paper towel for each window. There was a system to be followed. Erica was annoyed by systems, unless they were hers.

Mike tossed the handful of paper towels toward the overflowing trash can next to the gas pump and one of the folded sheets teetered on the rim and floated to the ground. He bent to retrieve it and noticed something out of place, leaning against the concrete base of the tank. He picked it up and examined it. It was just a child's wallet, soft red plastic, with a spray of white and yellow daisies embossed on one side. It was empty of cash, and the photo plastics held only cutouts of dolls. He shrugged and absentmindedly tossed it on the dash and went to see what was keeping Erica.

She exploded out of the door as he approached.

"I don't know why the hell you can't be on time. I've got better things to do than hang around here after work." She got into the truck and slammed the door, hard.

He was defensive. "If you expect me to pick you up, you need to be ready and waiting. You weren't anywhere to be seen."

"That's because I went back inside to phone when you weren't here," she countered. "I'll be damned if I'm going to wait in the rain. And I don't understand why you turn off that damned cell phone after work. I just got your stupid answering message."

"Maybe I turn it off for a reason." Mike was aware of the involuntary grinding of his jaw joints. "Maybe I like some peace after work."

Erica glared straight ahead, silent, infuriated. She perched stiffly, both hands clutching her new red ostrich-skin purse. Mike had never seen the purse before. He had long ago given up trying to keep up with Erica's shopping sprees.

He turned off the highway onto their private access west of town. The road snaked through several vertical cuts in the ubiquitous grey rock. It was still raining, and the wipers flapped back and forth like idiot conductors trying to make music out of the rhythm.

"What the hell is this?" Erica yelled. Something hit Mike on his right cheek.

Hand to his stinging face, he braked and fishtailed to a stop facing one of the rock cuts.

"You dirty bastard," she shouted. "Who is she this time?"

Mike reached to retrieve the projectile which was wedged between the still-engaged brake and the floor of the truck. It was the child's wallet.

"Christ, Erica, I just picked it up when I was waiting for you." He rubbed his cheek. "It was lying by the gas pump. It probably belonged to some kid. Jesus."

"You liar. You bloody damned liar. That's why you were late again. I want to know who it is." It was a familiar accusation. Erica was always jealous, but truth be told, there was never anything real for her to be jealous about.

On the other hand, Mike was aware of the truth about his pretty dark-haired wife. His buddies had hinted, hoping to expose her. But he knew, anyway. He knew the smell of her cheating, and had caught her in many a lie. But he still loved her.

She grabbed the wallet and brandished it in his face. "Tell me. Right now. Who is she?"

His jaw muscles flexed again and he felt the flush of anger moving up his neck. It was just too much. "You whore," he lashed back. "Just because you screw around with every trucker you know."

She grabbed the wallet.

"You can go straight to hell." She got out and slammed the door and stood in front of the truck in the downpour. "I'm sick of your shit. Fuck off. Leave me alone."

Mike took his foot off the brake and jammed the accelerator to back up. The truck lurched ahead as he realized too late and with horror that the transmission was still in drive. The truck crushed Erica between the grill and the rock cut. A fountain of bright blood spurted from her mouth. She slumped forward onto the hood, into the red stain already being washed away by the rain. Her eyes were already dead. The red wallet was still in her hand, and Mike could see the sticky shine of her blood on it. He got out of the truck and pried the wallet from her fingers. He tossed it into the truck, and it slid wetly across Erica's new red ostrich-skin handbag. He grabbed a handful of wet-wipes from the container under the seat and cleaned his hands.

Strangely, he felt no panic. He crumpled the bloody wipes into a ball and tried to think what to do.

Forgettory

The art of forgetting, within reasonable bounds,
is as desirable an accomplishment as the development of keen memory.

Forgetting is not an accident; it's an effort of will-power.

The stronger our will-power,
the easier for us to blot the past from our conscious minds.

A good memory is most valuable
when accompanied by a good forgettory.

Wisconsin State Journal,
Editorial, Sept 15, 1923

chapter 14
Missing

By the time Mike Slesiuk returned to his shop the sun was beginning to set red and angry through the dregs of the rainstorm. He parked his truck on the wash pad in the rear. He went inside and took off his bloodied jeans and t-shirt and put on a clean pair of green coveralls. He folded the soiled clothing and took it outside to his burning barrel along with several oily rags and tossed in a match. He hauled the pressure washer outside and attached it to the tap.

The awfulness of what had happened worked into every corner of his thoughts. He forced the horror to back down and flicked on the pressure washer.

He started at the front of the truck, at the grill. Back and forth, up and down, back and forth, he forced the powerful stream of water deep into the chrome grate. He willed the terrible vision to depart from his consciousness. He turned his attention to the back of the truck and scoured the floor with the fierce stream. He returned to the grill and blasted it once again. The water sprayed back into his face and merged with his wretched tears.

The dreadful image began to recede. Finally he turned off the pressure washer and took it inside. He came out with two new brand-new chamois and polished the truck dry. Even in the late twilight, it gleamed.

With his freshly washed truck, Mike Slesiuk pulled into the Country Gas Bar and Convenience Store west of Kenora. It was just after eleven, and the rain had finally dwindled to nothing. He parked in his usual spot around at the side of the store and went inside.

Mike and Erica were well known at the gas bar and convenience store. The owner, Don McKay, was married to Erica's younger sister Lil. Don often referred travelers with engine problems to Slesiuk Auto Repair, and if people asked about where there was a good place to eat he always sent them to Aunt Maggie's Truck Stop.

"Hi Mike. How's it goin'?" Don was sweeping the floor behind the counter. There was no one else in the store.

"Good. Have you seen Erica tonight?"

"No, I haven't." Don called into the small office at the back where his wife was doing up the late shift's cash. "Lil, was Erica in tonight?"

"Haven't seen her. Why?"

Mike drew his brow into a frown. "I dropped her off at the mall after work and she was going to get a ride home with one of her friends. I thought she would have been home hours ago. She's not answering her cell."

"She'll show up. Likely stopped in at the bar for a cooler." Don gathered his sweepings and scooped them into a yellow dustpan. "You might as well have a coffee. You can phone home in a while and see if she's there."

Through the rain they could make out a dark-coloured car pulling up to the gas pump.

"Never fails, does it?" Don grumbled. "I hate these buggers that pull in just as I'm about to shut everything down. Nine times out of ten they have some kind of problem and it sure pisses Lil off when she has to re-do the close-out."

Mike nodded. "Happens to me at the garage, too. But what can you do? It's business, right?"

The driver got out and selected unleaded and started to fill his tank. Don watched on the inside display as the man overrode the shutoff several times. Finally he finished and hurried into the store. He paid with a Master Card and bought some gum as an afterthought on his way out.

Don crossed to the door and turned the deadbolt and shut off the outdoor lights and the pumps. He poured two overripe coffees and they went into the small office at the back of the store where they waited with Lil to hear from Erica.

Mike was genuinely worried. "I can't understand why she hasn't called," he said.

chapter 15
Opportunity

Jervis Strunk was in a hurry. He had a productive evening in Kenora and Keewatin but he had learned the importance of putting fast space between himself and his activities. He was in too much of a hurry at first to stop for gas, but by the time he arrived at the Country Gas Bar and Convenience Store on the east side of town the old Ford was running on fumes. Only two other vehicles were parked in the lot, both near the coffee shop, a car and a truck.

Jervis eased the Ford up to the closest pump. He selected "unleaded" and thrust the nozzle in the tank, squeezing hard. He leaned back against the car and watched the lights of the scant traffic skim along the still-wet highway.

The face of the little girl he saw at the truck stop earlier in the day floated up in his mind. He remembered the deja-vue and suddenly realized it was the same face he had seen on the top copy of the bundle of newspapers beside the counter in the truck stop. Most of the headline had been obscured, but he now remembered part of it: *Have You Seen…* The child had reminded him of his younger sister Sierra. He should tell someone he saw the missing child. He deliberated for a very short moment and considered the contents of his car. It would be too risky to his own operations to go to the police. He again leaned back against the car.

The nozzle's automatic shut-off clicked and he overrode it several times. The gas overflowed, spilling on his new black western boots.

"Shit." He pulled out the nozzle and stepped back and kicked the gas pump. "Shit."

He chose a credit card from the pile in his glove compartment and shoved it into his pocket before entering the convenience store.

A tall man emerged from a room at the back.

"That be everything, pal?"

Jervis nodded and handed the card to the man. This was always the moment of truth. If the card was not accepted, or if the cashier questioned it (either eventuality was rare), Jervis would simply make his excuses and pay in cash.

The man ran the card through the machine and returned it to Jervis without examining it. Jervis scribbled an unintelligible signature on the receipt and stuffed the card back into his pocket. As an afterthought he bought a package of Juicy Fruit gum with a five-dollar bill.

Once outside he checked around carefully. A circle of orange light surrounded the pump area but the coffee shop cast a dark shadow over the parking lot on the east side. The car and truck stood parked in the semi-darkness. The man inside the convenience store had disappeared from the counter and there was no discernible movement inside the building.

Jervis drove back out toward the service road. Once out of sight of the coffee shop windows he killed his headlights and doubled back into the lot. He pulled up on the far side of the first vehicle, a car. Both the car and truck were unlocked. He shone his newly acquired red flashlight into the vehicles. The car had nothing to offer, but in the truck he found a dark red leather handbag and a wallet on the floor in front of the passenger seat. He grabbed both in one hand and threw them into the back seat of his car. He headed once more for the exit road.

The handbag reeked of cloying floral perfume and the scent filled the car. It reminded Jervis of fragments of something beyond of his range of recall. Ropes of twisted rags. Long dirty black hair. The sour smell of old urine. Vomit. Excruciating pain. Hunger. Cold. A familiar surge of hate and rage rose up from the thick floral scent and surrounded him and suffocated him.

chapter 16
Survival

Child and Family Services said it was one of the worst cases of neglect they had ever seen.

A neighbour had reported the incessant screaming of an infant. It had been going on for two days straight, she said. When the social workers arrived they found a severely malnourished three-month-old boy who still managed the pitiful strength to cry aloud. Alone in the cold and squalid apartment, he lay in a stinking cloth diaper that did not appear to have been changed for days. The rash beneath the diaper oozed with blood and pus. The social workers removed him immediately to a foster home. It took them two more days to locate his mother, Mandy Strunk, who was found thoroughly stoned in a downtown hotel room. But for the neighbour, the infant would surely have died.

Little Jervis Oswald Strunk thrived in foster care. The only residual effect of his shocking neglect was his raspy voice. He had screamed so hard for so long that his tiny vocal cords were permanently damaged.

Mandy Strunk reappeared to claim Jervis when he was four. By all accounts she seemed to have reformed. There was a live-in boyfriend, Dan, who had been around for over two years. They lived in a decent little apartment on Lipton Street in Winnipeg's west end, and there was another child, a two-year-old girl named Sierra. Child and Family Services deemed that Mandy was sufficiently rehabilitated to have Jervis returned to her care.

As long as Dan was in the picture there were no problems, but he walked out shortly after Jervis's return. No one seemed to notice that Mandy was alone with the children. For that matter, few people even realized she had children. They were never seen. No one paid any attention when she entertained men every night of the week, and the government agency overseeing the family was stretched too thin to bother calling on anyone without overt problems.

Mandy blamed little Jervis for Dan's departure and she focused her fury on the child. There was no one to see when she locked him in a closet for days on end. He survived on rotting scraps of food and learned how to swallow the nausea down so he would not be forced to eat his own vomit. The stench in the closet permeated his skin and his hair. His eyes oozed with infection, as did the cigarette burns on his arms and legs. When Mandy did allow Jervis out of the closet, she bound his hands and feet with strips of rag. Jervis came to prefer the closet. At least there he didn't have to endure the pain of the burns or the bruises of being beaten with a piece of one-inch dowel or the hair-pulling that left patches of his scalp bare. He preferred the eye-watering reek of the closet to the heavily cloying cologne with which Mandy doused herself.

The little girl Sierra suffered too, but not in the ways Jervis did. Sierra was malnourished and dirty and bruised but was allowed to move about in the apartment. She scrounged for food and brought bits and scraps to Jervis, who would probably have died without her. The children had a bond. It was the closest thing either knew to what might be described as a human relationship. When Mandy was out, Sierra crawled into the closet with Jervis where the two lay close together for warmth. At the sound of Mandy's key in the door, Jervis would frantically push Sierra out of their stinking nest. She had been caught in the closet once, and received a beating that left her with a cracked rib and a face so bruised and swollen she couldn't open her eyes or mouth.

The sheer will to survive kept Jervis's heart beating in his ever-diminishing body, but it was an impossible ordeal. For three years the abuse and neglect continued.

One night an insistent heavy banging roused the children in the closet. Sierra had been warned to never let anyone in but she edged into the kitchen and stood close to the door. Mandy always kept the door locked, but on this occasion she had forgotten. Sierra froze as the door eased open and a thin bearded face poked into the kitchen.

"Holy stinkin' shit," said the mouth under the beard. "Where the hell did you come from?"

Child and Family Services arrived within an hour of the man's telephone call. Jervis and Sierra were placed in foster care. They were separated, and the last memory Jervis had of Sierra was of her long hair blowing in the April wind as she was led away from him. He was too weak to call her name. He never saw her again. But every time he sees a girl around the age of five or six with long dark hair he imagines it is Sierra, even though he knows she would be in her early twenties by now.

Jervis was moved into a foster home. It was in Brandon, run by a couple who had no children of their own. They were good foster parents, as good as anyone could have been when dealing with such a severely damaged child. For the first time in his life Jervis was fed regular meals and tucked into a warm bed every night and allowed to sit close to the softness of his foster mother while he watched television. He was secure, at least on the surface. When he started school in the fall he was going on eight years old in the first grade. No one would have been able to tell his age by looking at him, as he was thin and small for his age. He completely lacked the ability to interact with the other children. His damaged voice rasped like sandpaper. And then there was his name—Jervis Oswald Strunk. One can only imagine why a mother would choose to give a child such an ugly combination of names. *Nervous Jervis. Strunk stunk. Skunk Strunk Stunk.* The bullying started almost immediately and continued throughout his school years. He told no one. His teachers were complicitly guilty of allowing it to happen.

There is no escape from a pecking order. In the animal world bullying is common. It is done as part of a species survival mechanism. Animals and birds cull the weak and sickly members of their herds and flocks and drive them to the outer edges of the social order. There they die or are left behind or become the easy victims of predators.

Some of them manage to exist on the fringes of the social order. They learn to survive on their own. They take what they need and they contribute nothing in return. This was Jervis—a lone wolf trailing along just out of sight of the rest of the pack.

He was a relatively good-looking man in an understated, forgettable sort of way. He was short, never having recovered from the stunting effect of his early years. He had learned to be charming when he needed to. But below Jervis Oswald Strunk's ordinary-looking surface boiled a soulless rage.

MARGARET RIDDELL

chapter 17
Almost Home

Sixteen-year-old Jodie Brightsky was almost home.

Less than twelve hours earlier she had scribbled a goodbye note to Tina on the back of a pizza flyer before making her way to Regina's Victoria Avenue. She trudged west to the outskirts of the city before turning to face the traffic with her thumb. Her long hair blew around her face and she pulled it back to the nape of her neck and secured it with a red hair elastic. It was just before noon.

The runaway adventure had been a two-year debacle. Jodie Brightsky's degraded body and soul ached for sanctuary.

From the beginning, the whole thing had been Tina's idea. Tina was Jodie's best friend—the charismatic leader, the grand planner, the decision maker. Jodie followed Tina like an obedient shadow. Tina was exciting. She was fun.

"Don't you want to get out of this boring hole?" Tina had prodded. "There's nothing to stay around here for."

Jodie resisted at first, but Tina was hard to deny.

"Running away would be cool," Tina laughed. "Let's just do it."

They could stay with Tina's cousin Johnny in Regina at first. He knew people who would look after them, Tina said, people who wouldn't tell where they were, who would let them do whatever they wanted. What Tina didn't understand was that the girls would be expected to earn their keep.

And now, Jodie Brightsky was going home. The benign trucker who picked her up just outside of Regina stopped at a roadside café near Indian Head and bought her a cheeseburger and fries. He took her all the way to the Ste. Anne exit east of Winnipeg. A Mennonite farmer in a dusty green van dropped her off at a rest stop near the Ontario border. She washed her face and hands in the restroom and removed the red elastic band, letting her hair fall around her shoulders. She extracted a chocolate bar from the vending machine and ate it outside at a picnic table. She overheard two elderly fishermen in the parking lot talking about heading north for some early angling at Minaki, and she approached them. They agreed to give her a ride to the Minaki Junction, and deposited her there just after eleven. They were concerned about leaving her on the highway late at night but she assured them she would be fine.

She knew exactly where she was. She was almost home. Hitch-hiking did not always end well, Jodie knew, and she had been fortunate. Now, there was only one short leg left in her journey. One more ride.

The floral fragrance from the red purse filled Jervis Strunk's nostrils. Fury boiled in his veins. An erection pushed painfully into the zipper of his jeans. His white knuckles wrapped around the steering wheel and beads of sweat covered his face as if they had been sprayed there.

And in the glare of his high beams, like a vision, he saw Jodie Brightsky. Her long dark hair blew around her face. She extended her arm to the road.

Jervis Strunk urgently needed to clean his car. He had dumped the girl already, along with her belongings and the dusty junk from the floor of the back seat. There was a self-serve carwash back past the truck stop, he remembered. But even more pressing was his urgent need for a shower. Campgrounds were his facility of choice; they all had restrooms and showers. Most were free to campers, but as far as Jervis could tell no one ever checked people coming and going with towels and shower bags.

For a long time he stood under the almost-hot stream of water, lathering himself with Irish Spring, breathing in the clean scent and clearing his nostrils of the remnants of the cloying perfume of the previous night. He wrapped himself in his navy towel and spread the contents of his shower bag on the narrow shelf below the mirror. He applied spray deodorant before shaving with a safety razor. Finally, he dressed in the clean jeans and grey t-shirt he had brought from the suitcase in the trunk of his car. He gathered his belongings and made his way to the visitors' parking area near the entrance of the campground.

He was careful to exit the campground by a different road than the one he had used to enter. He thought it would probably not take more than five minutes to make his way back to the carwash.

Jodie Brightsky lay at the side of a pathway leading to the restrooms. The first slanting sunlight of the day stretched sharp shadows across her naked body. A rolled pile of torn and bloodied clothing lay a few feet from her, in the midst of a scattering of dirty rags and miscellaneous trash. Her open red backpack sprawled behind her, spilling out sneakers and underwear and cheap make-up.

She forced the swollen slits of her eyes to open and tried to understand the gravel so close to her face. The events of the night before were like a dream that recoiled in pain as soon as it was touched. She remembered stepping into the darkness of some kind of vehicle. She had a fleeting sense of searching, clutching for something to hold on to.

She shivered convulsively. She strained to swallow the stinking taste in her mouth and her bruised and swollen throat gagged. She could hear sounds of slow traffic grumbling from close by. She crawled to the rolled pile and shook out her jeans and torn white T-shirt. Her movements awakened clouds of mosquitoes as she struggled into the clothing.

A wallet fell from the pile of rags. Holding the torn clothing together with one hand, she bent to pick up the wallet. She staggered into the restroom and splashed cold water on her bruised face. She wiped the wallet with a dampened paper towel and placed it on the vanity near one of the sinks. It might be evidence, she thought.

Her knees buckled beneath her. Jodie Branson was aware of the chill of cold tiles on her cheek just before blackness folded in around her.

MARGARET RIDDELL

chapter 18
Nipigon

Beyond the turnoff to Pass Lake, two police cars with flashing lights surged over a slight rise in the highway. Their sirens, shrieking like banshees of death, dopplered towards Finn and on past into the sodden darkness behind him. He glanced at his speedometer. His speed was well within the limits. He slowed a little, just to be safe.

For a short distance this stretch of the Trans-Canada runs between the CN and CP rail lines. In all the times he had been over this road Finn had never seen traffic on either track, but this time there were freight trains on both sides of him. They travelled in opposite directions, and Finn had the sensation of moving in a vast time warp. The motion sickened him and he slowed down and pulled onto the shoulder of the highway and waited until both trains were gone. He retrieved a Red Bull from the refrigerator in the sleeper cab and chain-smoked two Exports before pulling back onto the road. There was little traffic after ten thirty and the rain eased up as Finn neared Nipigon. The lights of a Tim Horton's beckoned just ahead and he decided to pull in to the drive-through for an extra-large triple-triple. Back on the highway, he watched for the side road that led to Squeaky Chubaty's place. In the high beam of his headlights the weather-beaten sign poked through tall grass at the edge of the road. With letters missing like lost teeth, it pointed the way to SQU AKY'S APPL IANCE SA ES & ERVICE. Weeds obscured the telephone number. Finn glanced at the dashboard clock. Eleven ten. Right on time.

Squeaky Chubaty raised the scarred metal door of his large windowless Quonset and Finn backed his rig up to the dock and rolled up the door. He entered the shed through a side door. A menacing growl erupted and segued to vicious barking as soon as he set foot on the concrete floor of the shed.

Squeaky thought this was funny. "What's the matter, Brute? Hey, boy, this is Finn! You remember Finn?"

Finn hoped so. The growling continued and came closer.

Brute responded with a cacophony of guttural growls and barks. "Shut the fuck up, dog!" Squeaky planted a kick on Brute's rump. The dog let out an injured yelp and edged closer to Finn, sniffing in short hot breaths. He pushed his huge marled head under Finn's hand and his crooked tail started to slap back and forth. Finn exhaled.

"Hey, Brute, can you smell your brother? Can you smell Arturo?" The dog snorted and rooted his nose under Finn's elbow like a pig. His skinny tail whipped back and forth.

Arturo had been Brute's littermate, given to Finn by Squeaky two years earlier. Both animals were marled grey-white with ice-blue eyes set in heads like cinder bricks, and had necks and shoulders that would have made a wrestler envious.

Arturo existed on Finn's stony farm in an inescapable chain-linked pen large enough for a dozen dogs. There was always plenty of dry food in a trough-style box under a lean-to shelter, and Finn usually remembered to fill the half-barrel with water before he left on a road trip. Once in a while the dog might get lucky and get a box of bones from the slaughter house if Finn had had a steer killed for beef, but other than that, Arturo was on his own. Finn thought nothing of leaving the animal alone for days at a time. Made him tough, Finn said.

Brute continued to root at Finn's arm while Squeaky dug a couple of Molson's out of the grubby-looking refrigerator in the back corner of the shed. He handed one to Finn.

"So, good trip down? No hitches?"

"Yeah, no problems. Lots of shitty rain."

"Been pouring here all day, too. Just stopped. How were the scales?"

"You know those assholes. Most of them, you could put a freight train past them and they wouldn't notice. The washers and dryers are perfect."

"You stop at Thunder Bay for your usual, uh…piece of cake?

"Nah, she wasn't working tonight. Just as well. She's starting to get bossy."

Squeaky laughed and drained his Molson.

"Might as well get started here."

He started his loader and pulled up to the dock.

Finn climbed into the back of the trailer and rolled the two front crates out of the way. They held a new washer and dryer set, unopened. The remaining eight crates appeared to be identical to the first two. Squeaky eased them out of the trailer and onto the floor. He cut the metal strapping and pried the tops off the boxes and peered into each one with a flashlight.

"Looks good, pal. Honda, Subaru, Dodge Ram. Just what we ordered."

"Yep, here's the list. You'll be happy. Moggey didn't have a lot of time to pull all this together, but he did a real good job.

There's a couple of crates he's still working on, has some VIN plates to remove, airbag extractions, so on. I'll bring them down with the next load."

"Where the hell did you find a guy like Andy Moggey, anyway?"

"Shit, known him for years. He used to work in a body shop in Gimli. We got talking one day about a pair of old trucks I chopped and reassembled when I was a kid, and one thing led to another. He was looking for a better deal for himself and I had just got rid of the livestock part of my trucking operation, and it just came together. Works for both of us."

Squeaky moved the crates to the back of the shed with a forklift and returned with two more beers. Brutus settled down at Finn's feet under the widening haze of Export smoke. Finn finished his beer in one long pull.

"Eleven thirty. Guess we better get the return freight on the road."

He climbed into the trailer and began the careful process of unlocking the almost invisible compartments that lined the sides, each just wide enough to accommodate a stack of contraband cigarettes. Squeaky piled the plastic-wrapped packages on the dock and then helped Finn pack the walls of the trailer. Once the compartments were full each panel locked with a pressure sensitive latch on the third rivet from the top of the section. The barely visible compartments were Andy Moggey's work, and perhaps his most polished accomplishment. Finally, Finn rolled the two crates with the washer and dryer back into their place in the trailer and lowered the door.

Squeaky scratched his butt. "Safe trip back, pal." He pressed a small box into Finn's hand. "Here's something for the road."

chapter 19
Impairment

Layers of mist settled into the low places on the highway. The air was still. Finn watched the yellow lines disappear in staccato flashes beneath the front of his truck. Now and then the lines became a solid stream and sometimes a combination of flashes and streams. Finn topped a rise in the road and watched the markings disappear into a flat froth of white at the bottom of the downward slope. When he drove down into the froth the lines reappeared, but now they were writhing, merging into one another, twisting like shining golden snakes in white mist. Finn started up the other side of the dip in the road, and the snakes rolled and raced ahead of him.

Finn's head pounded and his eyelids felt like they were lined with hot ashes. He reached for the Advil in the console and twisted open the lid with the finger and thumb of one hand. He tipped the container to his mouth and felt three or four gels slide over his tongue. The rest of the gels in the bottle scattered to the floor of the truck when he tried to replace the lid. He washed the Advil down with a swig of Red Bull. The highway lines continued to roll and waver. Finn was certain he could see hundreds of glowing animal eyes flickering on the shoulder of the road.

Just west of Kakabeka Falls Finn pulled the rig into a rest stop, but not for a rest. He didn't need that. He went back into the sleeper and used his turd-burner before stepping out into the parking lot for an Export. There were four other rigs parked at the stop. Three truckers were sleeping, Finn surmised, and the fourth was involved in an altercation with a young woman. Finn watched him drag the woman from the cab and slap her in the face and head several times before throwing her to the ground. The woman struggled to her feet and began running towards the highway, the trucker in pursuit. Finn could hear her frantic voice but couldn't quite make out what she was saying. She stumbled up the incline of the ditch and fell on her knees just as the trucker caught up to her. He yanked her to her feet and dragged her back to the truck and shoved her head-first back into the cab. Finn considered intervening but decided better of it. He couldn't afford to get involved. He needed to get back on the road.

The highway lines continued their winding dance beneath the eighteen wheels of Finn's rig. Signs flashed by—Shebandowan, Raith, Upsala, English River, Ignace—Finn oblivious to all of them. But he sat up straight and took notice when he saw the passenger train crossing the highway just ahead of him, its windows all alight. It was close, so close that he doubted he would be able to avoid crashing into it. As he neared the point of impact the train morphed into a row of reflector lights marking the curve in the highway. The double yellow lines sucked Finn around the bend and left him, rattled, still headed west.

Fortuitous circumstance had Finn approaching Dryden in the pre-dawn lightening just as the beeping alarm of the fuel tank indicator indicated an urgent need for a refueling stop. There was a cardlock in Dryden where he filled his tanks before stopping at the nearby Tim Horton's for a large 4x4 and a twenty-pack of Timbits.

chapter 20
Last Leg

Katie Maybank and John Lindblom rose earlier than usual, anxious to put the last leg of their truncated cross-Canada trip behind them. The rain had stopped sometime in the night but the tent and gear were still soggy. They went through the camp-breaking routine that had become so familiar in the past weeks. Neither spoke. Their bikes were loaded with four panniers each; one of John's held Katie's excess clothing.

Backpacks in hand, they headed for their respective wash-rooms. An attendant was busy swabbing the floor in the women's facility. Katie had to step over the sour-smelling string mop to get to the sinks, which had not yet been cleaned. She chose the least grimy of the three and waited for it to fill with water that offered only a hint of warmth. A small red plastic wallet lay on the counter between the sinks. It had a vague familiarity.

"Someone left a wallet here," Katie said to the attendant. "Did you see anyone in here this morning?"

The attendant shrugged. "No, I don't think so. Well, unless you count the ambulance people. They took a girl away from here a while ago. Unconscious."

Katie opened the wallet. There was no identification inside, nothing but pictures cut from magazines, or perhaps catalogues. Pictures of dolls. She showed it to the attendant.

"Looks like it might've belonged to a little kid," the attendant mumbled. "You might as well take it." She poked the filthy mop around the supporting legs of the toilet stalls. "Nobody ever claims junk like that."

Katie remembered where she had seen the wallet once before. A little girl in a tantrum had thrown it to the floor of yesterday's restaurant. Katie tucked it into the back pocket of her jeans. She looked around the squalid washroom and shuddered, hoping the little girl had not been the one taken away by the ambulance. She pulled the wallet out of her pocket and opened it again. Besides the paper cut-outs, there was a torn piece of paper tucked in a different compartment. Crayon lettering spelled out ESL111 on the scrap. It looked like a licence plate number. That was all. Katie couldn't shake the feeling that something might have happened to the girl.

"Hurry up, Katie. Let's get this show on the road." John's voice, louder than necessary, Katie thought, came from right outside the washroom door.

She tucked the wallet back into her pocket. *I'll deal with this when we get to Winnipeg. I'll have to let someone know.*

The cyclists laboured to the top of a gentle hill between limestone walls on one side and rocky outcrops of pink and brown granite on the other. The rain-washed air was heavy with the fragrance of hundreds of flowers poking through the short roadside grasses. The panorama reminded Katie of one of her favourite paintings by Elise Kot—tall stalks of bluebells, bright golden buttercups clinging tenaciously to the rocky shoulder, tiny asters in varying shades of pink and mauve, white daisy fleabane, black-eyed Susans and dainty purple vetch trailing itself along wherever its tendrils decided to take it.

John studied the limestone outcrop on the other side of the road, admiring the way its once-perfect horizontality now slanted and curved where it had been lifted by great slow lava flows. Higher up on the limestone he could make out the outline of a small fossil of some kind, and he saw in his mind the ancient ocean that had once covered the land.

They rested at the top of the hill a few more moments, then pushed off for the lazy descent. Both of them felt a sense of relief, a lifting of weight. It was a beautiful morning. The relationship was over and admitted. Just over the hill, Katie stopped to adjust a small imbalance in one of her panniers and ahead, John waited for her to catch up.

chapter 21
Apparition

Finn Erikson always liked driving west in the morning. He adjusted his mirror to avoid the low sun behind and opened a Red Bull to wash down a pair of bennies from the packet Squeaky gave him. He was proud of himself. Winnipeg to Nipigon and return, non-stop except for meals, no problem. He yawned and stretched. *Some guys would be hallucinating by now. But not Finn Erikson.* He turned up the radio volume another notch and decided to bypass Aunt Maggie's Truck Stop. He would visit with Erica on another trip, hopefully when he had more time.

In Finn Erikson's unblinking stare, a spiral of colored smoke passed over the rise in the highway ahead. He followed the swirl. It writhed and twisted, and shiny glints of white fire flashed from within. Finn tried to understand, to classify the apparition. It had stopped moving, and he could see that his truck was about to pass right through the beautiful mists. As he slammed into the coloured cloud he was aware of a scrambling of metal and of something else tangling beneath his wheels.

Flying debris filled the air—sunglasses, shoes ripped from feet, touring maps, metal camping dishes, a cell phone, one white leather glove, a paperback book, a small wallet. The debris seemed to suspend itself above the highway for a moment before it spun and clattered and spread itself across the pavement and the gravel shoulders and the narrow ditch.

Finn Erikson was now fully awake. He braked frantically and tried to shift down through the truck's gears. His rig jackknifed and drifted sideways and came to a scraping halt next to a tall outcropping of limestone at the side of the highway. Shaken and now abundantly conscious, Finn loosened his white-knuckled grip on the gear stick and the steering wheel. The limestone cut hung just outside his driver's side window. *For a good time call Anita,* he read on the rock just inches from his sweating face, noting that the promising telephone number had disappeared below the truck's door. And on the pavement and in the ditches behind Finn Erikson and his truck, his passage was blazed by a stretch of bloody debris and mangled bits of metal and scattered belongings.

Passing vehicles from both directions quickly collected around the scene. People could not resist the temptation to get out and gape at the carnage. A woman in a Nine Inch Nails tee shirt screamed hysterically at the sight of a severed hand on the road next to her car. Someone had the presence of mind to call 911. A tall red-headed man with some common sense tried to route the traffic on its way and most drivers complied.

Finn slouched low in his truck and stared unblinking, unfocused, at the wide, bright highway ahead of him.

chapter 22
Aftermath

Following the accident with the cyclists Finn Erikson spent one afternoon in jail in Kenora. The first thing he did was to call his lawyer Garth Minton in Winnipeg. Minton made a connection with an Ontario colleague who managed to get Finn out on bail the following morning. Finn's partner Andy Moggey drove down from Winnipeg to pick him up and bring him home.

There was nothing in Finns impeccable trucker's log that was remotely incriminating, but a search of his truck and personal effects turned up diesel and restaurant receipts which proved he had been on the road for at least twenty hours. There were only trace amounts of alcohol in his blood, but he was unable to perform even the simplest of sobriety tests. Toxicology tests revealed a sky-high reading for barbiturates in his system. His driver's licence was suspended until trial. Finn's truck was impounded and eventually returned to Winnipeg. When the truck jack-knifed and scraped in to the wall of rock at the scene of the accident, Andy Moggey's inventive false lining cracked. Contraband cigarettes spilled onto the floor of the trailer, adding to the litany of charges against Finn.

Finn Erikson's case took a year to work its way through the court system. He was charged with Unintentional Vehicular Manslaughter, and in a separate indictment, with smuggling contraband tobacco. While he waited, he and Moggey continued their illicit auto parts business with the help of Moggey's brother Pete and their Nipigon connection, Squeaky Chubaty. Finn was never entirely comfortable with Marcus Nagel, the truck driver Moggey recruited to run the trips to Ontario, but Marcus performed well. The OPP watched Squeaky for a while but never found anything in his run-down Quonset other than large appliances in various states of disrepair. There was an old paper trail to Finn Erikson and it verified the delivery and pickup of washers and dryers and occasional refrigerators over a period of about three years. There were no leads to illicit tobacco.

When Finn's case finally hit the docket it lasted less than a week, and netted Finn ten thousand dollars in fines and consecutive sentences of ten and five years in prison for the charges of manslaughter and tobacco smuggling. It was to be served at the Stony Mountain Penitentiary. The echo of the judge's gavel had barely died out when Finn's lawyer Garth Minton started to work on an appeal.

chapter 23
Crossing The Line

Even at nine in the morning, the lineup at the Niagara Falls border crossing was stretched back at least a quarter of a kilometer at all gates. With its windows down, the red Subaru inched forward in its lane.

Her hands sticky with sweat, the woman fussed with the documents. She inspected the passports and the birth certificate once again as if they might somehow have changed since the last time she checked everything ten minutes earlier. Ahead, they could see a car being pulled aside for inspection. She stacked the documents and held them tightly. The man drummed his fingers on the steering wheel and they crept forward again. They had been in line only twenty minutes but it seemed it had been much longer by the time they reached the windowed cubicle.

The woman handed the passports and birth certificate to the man and he in turn passed them to the border inspector, who examined them for a time-stretched moment. Still holding the documents, he leaned out of his kiosk a little and studied the man and woman. He could see the child in the back seat, curled up against the far door like a nervous kitten.

"Where are you from?"

"Saskatoon." The man felt uneasy with this answer, but that was what the passport indicated.

"Are you all Canadian citizens?"

"Yes, sir."

"What is the purpose of your trip?"

"We're on vacation."

"Where will you be staying?"

"We're headed for Disneyworld, in Florida. The Lake Buena Vista."

"And how long will you be in the U.S.?"

"We'll be home the end of July. Three weeks."

"How much money are you carrying?"

"A thousand dollars, maybe a bit less. And credit cards."

"Do you have any drugs or alcohol or weapons?"

"No, sir."

"Is this vehicle registered to you?"

"Yes, it is."

"May I see the registration, please?"

The man reached over and opened the glove compartment. He was nervous; he had never been asked for the registration in the many times he had crossed the border. He took the papers out of the plastic sleeve and handed them to the inspector, who studied everything closely. He was glad he had given Saskatoon as his address instead of Winnipeg. It matched the registration. The inspector handed back the papers.

He squinted into the back seat.

"What's your name?" he asked the child.

She pulled herself further into the corner.

"Can you please tell me your name?"

The woman leaned over the back seat. "It's all right, sweetie. You have to tell him your name. Don't be shy."

The child pulled her t-shirt up over her mouth.

"Emily," she whispered.

The little voice hung in the air like a sigh.

The inspector wrote something on a notepad on his counter. He handed the passports and birth certificate back to the man.

"Have a good vacation," he said, unsmiling, nodding for them to pass through.

Part Two

chapter 24
Janelle And Patrick

Janelle first met Patrick St. Clair at Zola-Rae Thompson's engagement party at the Green Gates Restaurant just west of Winnipeg. Zola-Rae's plans for a huge wedding were well underway and the event, she said, was primarily intended to introduce the members of the wedding party. Janelle accepted Zola-Rae's invitation to be maid of honour, heading up an assembly of six bridesmaids. Patrick St. Clair was the best man for the groom, Earl Bentley. Earl and Patrick had been best friends from the time they met in the Agriculture Faculty at the University of Manitoba.

The party was all about Zola-Rae, of course. She used the event as a platform to inform everyone about her (she never once said 'our') wedding plans. She had decreed the wedding was to be a black and white affair. That was exactly what would be expected of Zola-Rae—no grey areas. All invited guests would be expected to wear black or white or some combination of the two, with colourful accessories allowed, as long as they were red.

Zola-Rae displayed pictures of the dresses she had chosen for her attendants: gorgeous and elaborate two piece gowns with a sequined black layer over a white silk chemise. Janelle and the bridesmaids hinted that the expense of the dresses might be a hardship but there was no negotiating with Zola-Rae. *The gowns are already ordered*, she said. *Besides, I'm giving you lots of advance notice if you need to arrange a payment plan.*

She went on to talk at length about the flowers and the cake and the photographer and the invitations and the dinner menu and the dance. After a while the only one listening was Earl. The members of the wedding party, overwhelmed by the magnitude of her preparations, had succumbed to their wandering minds.

If it had been Zola-Rae's intention for the attendants to get to know each other, she failed miserably. They hardly had a chance to speak to each other over the torrent of details.

The next time Janelle and Patrick met was at Zola-Rae's next project: a social. She and Earl booked a hall at Southpoint for late May and six hundred tickets went on sale immediately. On the afternoon of the event the wedding party showed up as bidden to set up the hall. At the back, long tables overflowed with items for a silent auction. The items were mostly donated, some from family members and relatives, some from the wedding party, many from local businesses in Morris, which was Earl's home town. Gift certificates abounded, many of them tucked into baskets of assorted items. The items were numbered, with a corresponding brown paper bag taped to the table in front of each. Guests would buy numbered tickets for the auction and drop them into the bags of their choice. At the end of the evening, a draw would be made from each bag to determine the "winner" of each article. The silent auction was becoming an extremely lucrative event for young couples.

There would also be 50/50 draws, sold by arms-lengths of tickets also to be used for various donated door prizes. The final draw of the evening was for a 27-inch television, donated by Zola-Rae's parents.

Patrick St. Clair's job was to pick up the liquor at the Liquor Commission and to set up the bar at the front end of the hall beside the stage. Another of Earl's friends, a weather-burned farmer from Morris, helped Patrick haul the many cases of beer and hard liquor and mix. For six hundred social tickets sold, it was a large order.

As fast as the men could unload the liquor, Janelle Carpenter and two bridesmaids organized it behind the bar. The rest of the wedding party divided themselves between setting up the auction table and preparing food for the midnight buffet. Those in the kitchen arranged platters of salami and kielbasa and stacks of rye bread and dishes of pickles and cheese, and shrouded everything with plastic. They stocked each table with chips and pretzels.

Everyone was exhausted from the afternoon's work, and Zola-Rae sent Earl to get the two cases of wine she had stashed in the kitchen. Six huge pizzas arrived at the main entrance to the hall. For the first time, the members of the wedding party were allowed to relax.

Janelle and Patrick perched on stools behind the bar, apart from the others. An immediate connection blossomed between the two of them. They were the first to leave.

The day before the actual wedding the entourage arrived en masse to carry out Zola-Rae's elaborate decorating plans. Black and white streamers, huge trees of balloons anchored through-out the hall, black tablecloths, tiny sparkling lights, hundreds of red candles, engraved place cards for every guest—only the red rose centrepieces were missing. Zola-Rae appointed Patrick and

Janelle to pick up all the flowers the next morning and to set up the centrepieces before lunch. Everyone was expected to be at the meeting hall of the church, in full wedding regalia, by three. The photographer was adamant they be on time.

To Zola-Rae's credit, the event was stunning with its black-and-white theme. The guests had complied with the dress requirements, except for Zola-Rae's entitled mother Brenda, who wore a long red dress. *Well,* she said, *red is allowed as an accessory. You did say that, Zolie.*

The reception hall could have been a set for some kind of fantasy movie. The DJ announced the first dance for the newly-weds, and they took the floor to the strains of the requested *Heaven.* The DJ allowed them half a minute before summoning the rest of the wedding party to the floor. Zola-Rae was so busy absorbing the scene and evaluating everyone's reaction that she barely noticed she was dancing with her new husband.

But Patrick and Janelle didn't see the black-and-white or the crowd or the fantastic décor. They only saw each other through the filter of the music. ...*once in your life you find someone who will turn your world around*...He brushed an errant strand of hair from her forehead. ...*Baby, you're all that I want*...

The evening drew to a close. The DJ called the wedding party to the floor for the last dance. He cued up REO Speedwagon's *Can't Fight This Feeling.* Released from their moorings, the black and white balloons floated and curled overhead, catching sparks of light from the glitter ball.

The rest of the wedding guests joined the dance. The lights faded on as the last notes of music died. There was a round of applause for Zola-Rae and Earl. They left the floor, scattering hugs on the way.

But Patrick and Janelle remained in the centre of the dance floor. Patrick dropped to one knee and extended his hand to Janelle. He lifted a tiny blue velvet box.

The entire room fell into a hush of surprise, a collective drawing of breath.

"I love you, Janelle. Will you marry me? Will you be the lady of my castle in Fantasy Land?"

The stillness in the hall deepened and stretched.

"Yes, Patrick. I will. Yes, yes!"

The crowd exploded with applause and cheers and closed in on Patrick and Janelle, smothering them with hugs and congratulations.

Upstaged, Zola-Rae and Earl watched from the sidelines. Zola-Rae was furious.

chapter 25
Golden Circle

Patrick farmed with his family in the Golden Circle of Manitoba, but he always jokingly referred to the area as Fantasy Land.

"Nothing is true there," he once said, "and everything is kind of weird."

The region had been known geographically for years as the Golden Circle. No one was sure why, because when viewed on a map the four towns it encompassed were situated on the corners of a near-perfect ten-mile square. Good gravel roads criss-crossed the diagonals of the square, like spokes from a hub. The Golden Circle was not the strangest designation though, as each town had a name that simply begged to be made fun of. Agate Hill, the largest of the four communities, sat deep in the flats of the shallow and wide valley of the Whitewater River without a hill in sight. An agate had never been found anywhere nearby, and the Whitewater River was, in most years, little more than a muddy trickle.

Another settlement sprang up where the Whitewater Creek flowed into the Lumber River. There was no tree as far as could be seen. In the early days, lumber may have been shipped down the river, but no one remembered and most doubted the shallow stream would have supported any kind of barge. The Lumber River faded into a reedy marsh just outside the town.

Directly across the diagonal from Lumber River, the village of Crystal Lake grew and spread on the dry and treeless flatlands above Whitewater Creek. The only body of water within imagination might have been a glistening prairie mirage. Still, Crystal Lake still had a beautiful mural of a wide shining lake painted on the side of its municipal storage shed.

And on the final corner of the square of the Golden Circle sat Pelican Island, the smallest of the four towns. Without a nearby lake, there were no pelicans and definitely no islands. A small rise in the land could conceivably been an ancient island in Lake Agassiz, but that required quite a stretch of creative visioning.

The St. Clair family was an oasis of ordinariness in the Golden Circle. Walter and Nordeen had two boys, Patrick and Aarin, and a daughter Christine. Walter was a quiet, well-liked man. He died when Patrick was ten and Nordeen carried on the business of running their farm near the town of Agate Hill. Nordeen was an astute businesswoman and had always been the undisputed superior commander of the St. Clair operation, even when Walter was alive.

Janelle Carpenter married Patrick St. Clair on Christmas Day, at the Conservatory in Assiniboine Park. Janelle's father Jerry was present to give his daughter away, and her mother Yvonne who lived in Lethbridge sent a telegram.

Janelle was able to arrange a transfer from her job at the Royal Bank on Portage West to the branch in Agate Hill. She and Patrick moved in (apprehensively) with Nordeen while they waited for their mobile home to be delivered and set up in the farmyard.

MARGARET RIDDELL

Their first order of business as a married couple was to tell Nordeen about the baby. She didn't even try to hide her displeasure.

"Patrick, how could you be so careless?"

Nordeen had still not recovered from her raw irritation about the wedding being held on Christmas Day, and that she had no say in any of the arrangements.

Nordeen was a difficult person. She could be hugely intimidating and was not well-liked in the community, but she worked hard and volunteered for everything and got things done, so she was usually named as the chairperson or the head convenor or the co-ordinator of whatever project was underway at the time. She was the president of the curling club, head of the renovating committee for the church addition, catering co-ordinator for the community hall and self-appointed accompanist for any event requiring music. She ran the Christmas craft sale and single-handedly canvassed for the local United Way. She had many minions and she micro-managed all of them.

The St. Clair house was an imposing three-storey brick mansion built in the late 1920's by Patrick St. Clair's grandfather, George. Nordeen always insisted she would never move from that house. *They'll have to carry me out,* she said. Her daughter Christine packed her things and left when she turned eighteen, and went to Saskatoon. Nordeen never spoke of Christine but Patrick remembered her fondly. He was sixteen when she left in a chaos of bitter words and recriminations. But Nordeen was determined to hang on to her sons, even if that meant tolerating a daughter-in-law.

In spite of Nordeen's pressure, Patrick insisted; the living arrangement was only temporary. Patrick was no pushover. He was a husband now, soon to be a father. He was not like his brother Aarin, who simply did as he was told.

The brand new 1200-square-foot luxury mobile home arrived in March. Janelle and Patrick were thrilled.

You'd never get me into one of those things, said Nordeen. *You'll be sorry.*

Jonathan was born late that summer. It was evident from the beginning that all was not well. He was only two days old when they found out about the congenital defect. The ventricles and atria of the baby's tiny heart strained to push the rhythm of life into his wee body. His skin turned ashy grey and his breathing gave way to rapid gasps. Little Jonathan was transferred from Agate Hill's tiny hospital to Children's Hospital in Winnipeg. To buy time, specialists inserted an IV into the tiny body and the drip of the medication marked the wait: hours, days, weeks.

He's a real trooper, Patrick said. *He's a little fighter. He'll make it.*

Nordeen blames Janelle. *Is there something like this in your family?*

Little Jonathan was on perpetual standby. Transplants don't just happen at the wishful snap of a finger. When "something transpires," as the doctor euphemistically put it, "time is of the essence." When the dominoes begin to tip, when other parents, somewhere, pass on the pulse of their genes in a quivering pearly-pink piece of flesh, a tiny open chest needs to be ready to accept the gift.

In the distant eastern city where Janelle and Jonathan were sent, there were no relatives upon whom they might have imposed a lengthy visit. They rented a sparsely furnished apartment close to the hospital. Patrick waited alone at home, refusing to move in with Nordeen while Janelle was away.

But a transplant did not come in time to save wee Jonathan.

It's just as well, Nordeen said. *He would never have had a normal life.*

Janelle returned to her job at the bank and Patrick struggled through the motions of farming. In time, the jagged edges of their grief wore off and they returned to themselves. Two years passed. Life reasserted itself.

It was a Tuesday, the second week of October, the day after Thanksgiving. Janelle and Patrick had celebrated the holiday at Nordeen's the day before.

But for this day, Janelle had planned an intimate dinner for just the two of them. Patrick didn't know it yet, but they had something to celebrate.

Janelle fussed with the last minute details. Barbecued back ribs, creamed corn, fat baked potatoes, Caesar salad, saskatoon pie—all his favorites—everything was perfect for the occasion.

Patrick was baling flax straw on the ridge land at the west end of the valley. He was late for dinner, and this was not unusual on a farm, but when two hours passed, Janelle called Aarin to go and check on him.

No one will ever know why Patrick stopped the tractor at that particular spot in the field. He was always extremely conscientious about the power take-off, so why would he have not disengaged it when he got off the tractor?

Aarin found Patrick caught in the baler near the twine arm. When the First Responders finally arrived (it only took them twelve minutes to get there) there was nothing they could do. They speculated that he was probably attempting to untangle a snarl or knot in the twine. His jacket and shirt were completely imbedded in the bale. Patrick had been drawn into the machine, too. The autopsy report declared the cause of death to be compression asphyxia.

Janelle never had the chance to tell him her good news.

chapter 26
Nellie

Nordeen St. Clair was in a state of high dudgeon when she was not allowed into the delivery room. She waited in the visitors' lounge with Janelle's father Jerry, who had consumed four shots of Crown Royal and was pleasantly able to shrug off Nordeen's ranting.

Janelle Patricia was named after her parents. She would be called Nellie.

Don't you think that's kind of old-fashioned for a little girl? Nordeen said.

Nordeen insisted on a baptism ceremony, and Janelle agreed; it was what Patrick would have wanted.

Grandma Yvonne Carpenter sent a congratulatory telegram from Lethbridge.

When Nellie was one, Janelle went back to work, this time at the Agate Hill Credit Union. Nordeen insisted on babysitting Nellie free of charge. Janelle had uneasy misgivings about the arrangement but decided to give it a try.

Nordeen was delighted to once again have a child to mold, and she proceeded with her usual audacity. She surreptitiously ignored Janelle's instructions about food and naps and clothing.

She refused to use the baby shampoo Janelle provided, allowed Nellie to eat peanut butter on salty crackers, and gave her sugared tea in a plastic cup. *It never hurt my kids,* she told her neighbour. *They grew up healthy.* When Nellie turned one, Nordeen instigated rigorous toilet training without Janelle's knowledge. She returned Nellie to Janelle at the end of each day with a litany of advice and instructions. Nellie appeared to be happy and well-cared for, so Janelle, unaware of much of what was happening, gritted her teeth and allowed Nordeen to carry on.

Nordeen took selfish pleasure in describing the details of all the "firsts" she was experiencing with Nellie—the little words, the first steps, and the self-feeding success with Patrick's silver baby spoon. Without actually putting it into words, she made it clear that Janelle was missing the milestones of Nellie's babyhood.

Janelle's co-worker, Cheryl Cotton, took her aside in the lunch room at the bank one day. "I don't know if it's my place to tell you," Cheryl said, "but if it was my child I'd want to know. Nordeen took Nellie to a catering meeting at the hall yesterday afternoon. My friend Alicia Winter, I think you've met her? Anyway, Alicia said that Nordeen left Nellie sleeping in the back seat of her car the whole time she was at the meeting. Alicia thought someone should tell you."

Janelle was shocked. She addressed the situation with Nordeen, who played down the incident.

"Pfft. Oh, for Lord's sake, Janelle, Alicia is always trying to make trouble. I was only in the hall for five minutes. It was nothing. The car was parked in the shade and the window was cracked. Nellie was just fine. And it isn't Alicia's business, or Cheryl's either."

But it is my business, Janelle bristled inwardly.

"I don't want you to leave Nellie in the car again, Nordeen."

Nordeen huffed away. "Hmph. If you say so."

Janelle was looking after Mrs. Widmore at her teller station the next day. Mrs. Widmore was always very chatty.

"I just want to tell you dear, I saw your little Patty the other day. She's such a beautiful child. Reminds me of Patrick when he was that age."

It took a moment for the comment to register. *Mrs. Widmore gets confused sometimes.* Janelle slid a paper across the counter for Mrs. Widmore to sign.

"Thank you, Mrs. Widmore. I'm so lucky to have her. But her name is Nellie."

Now Mrs. Widmore *was* confused.

"But I saw her with Nordeen at the Co-op. Nordeen said, this is my granddaughter Patty. This is Patrick's daughter, she said. I'm *sure* she said her name was Patty."

Janelle was fuming. When she picked Nellie up from Nordeen's at the end of the day, she clenched her teeth. She didn't mention the conversation with Mrs. Widmore.

She guessed it would take a couple of weeks to re-arrange her life. Nordeen would never know what hit her until it was too late for her to do anything about it.

Janelle moved back to Winnipeg with Nellie. Patrick's brother Aarin agreed to take over the mobile home but was sworn to secrecy until the day after Janelle left. Jerry Carpenter had an extra room in his apartment on Pembina Highway and offered to help with the cost of daycare. He put his bottles away. Having Nellie in his home was almost like having little Susan back again. Janelle got a job at her old bank—a better position than her previous one—and started work right away. Her hours allowed much more time to be spent with Nellie.

Janelle did keep in touch with Nordeen, once the fury wore off. Nordeen came to Winnipeg occasionally to see Nellie. She behaved very carefully in the wake of the circumstances. It made Janelle nervous.

Thief in the Light

It sneaks up undetected,
a brazen thief in the bright light of day.

It steals small to begin with: an expression,
a small memory, a recognition.

The losses are inconsequential,
barely noticed at first.

The thefts begin to accrue. Others begin to notice
the things that go missing—the recall of details of the past,
the words lost to the tip of the tongue,
the clarity of judgment.

It confiscates mental and physical ability,
communication, emotion and independence.
It strips away whatever tiny particle
may be left of the essence of humanity.

M.R.

chapter 27
Booker And Bonnie

Anyone who didn't know Booker and Bonnie Johnson would have found it difficult to imagine they had ever been anything but a dowdy old pair of seniors.

Booker was tall and straight and too thin. He was usually garbed in baggy grey pants and a short-sleeved button-down dress shirt. Sometimes he wore a ratty navy wool cardigan which had been a gift from his daughter Charlene who lived in England. His fading sandy hair was parted too low on the right and he combed the thin tendrils over the sparsely populated spot on top of his head. Ancient sneakers completed his attire.

Booker doddered along, eyes focused on the ground close to his feet. Bonnie herded him around corners and through doorways and to the dinner table and in and out of the car. Booker would not have been able to survive without his valiant little wife.

Bonnie had become solid and round with the passage of time. Her grey hair glinted of blue and was styled in the short curly-perm cookie-cutter style of so many women her age. Her wardrobe was almost exclusively TanJay—she owned dozens of very brightly patterned polyester shirts, each of which was coordinated with a pair of elastic-waist pants and topped off with matching beads. Some shirts had several pairs of matching pants. Bonnie's once-impeccable and expensive sense of style had evolved over the years into a quest for comfort and color. She was a physical complement to Booker.

But Booker and Bonnie were not always dowdy old seniors. They turned heads when they were young. Booker then sported a head of thick blond hair and intelligent dark eyes and wore expensive clothing on his muscular frame.

In those days Bonnie wore her dark hair in a striking upsweep and dressed in immaculate style, favoring deep blues and reds. Back then she was an avid volunteer in the community. She was the perfect counterpoint to the successful surgeon.

They were well-respected. They had earned their positions in society, and neither had allowed their wealth to interfere with their humanity.

Booker had humble beginnings. He was born in the family home at Birch Point and was raised as a farm boy, the fourth of ten children. Booker was a brilliant student. He burned through Grade Eleven when he was only fourteen years old and his teachers and parents decided it would be in his best interests to send him to a boarding school in Brandon. There he stretched his Grade Twelve over two years to get himself to an age where he was socially ready to take on the world. He filled in his spare time by participating in every sport he could find. He was still only sixteen when he attended Normal School for a year, and he faced his first students at the age of seventeen, in a tiny country school just west of Brandon.

Booker boarded at the home of a Brandon doctor who recognized his abilities and inspired him to pursue a career in medicine where his high marks ensured the awarding of many scholarships. He met Bonnie Ormiston at university when she volunteered as a spare for his curling team. Bonnie was studying to be a teacher. They married as soon as he completed his internship. Then the war interfered, and Dr. Booker Johnson joined the medical corps and was stationed in England while Bonnie taught a grade five class in St. James.

When he returned to Canada, he began a residency at a large hospital in Moncton, but he and Bonnie longed for the prairies. They moved back to Manitoba, to Winnipeg, and Booker returned to the University of Manitoba and studied to become a surgeon.

He established a very successful private practice and was well-known in the medical community, having pioneered cardiology techniques that were adopted around the world.

If there was an unfulfilled area of Booker and Bonnie's life, it would have to be that of family. Both had wanted to fill their home with children, but they were only able to conceive successfully on two occasions: Randy and Charlene.

Booker and Bonnie, as they say, lived a full life. They took up downhill skiing and canoeing, scuba diving and white-water rafting, snowmobiling and spelunking. Bonnie was an accomplished pianist and artist. They travelled—to Australia and Brazil and Hawaii and Europe and on a cruise to Alaska. They even went on an African safari one winter. They raised purebred spaniels and Booker built a boat. They had a cottage at Clear Lake and spent many summers there, especially when Randy and Charlene were children.

But Booker and Bonnie grew old. To anyone who did not know them, they looked like an eccentric pair of aging peasants. All the wonderful and exciting experiences of their lives were hidden behind their greying invisibility.

Dr. Booker Johnson's dementia progressed quickly following his first diagnosis. In the early stages he was aware of his condition and was able to function almost normally. Bonnie compensated for his confusion and memory lapses and helped him with conversations and set out their daily agenda. It wasn't until Booker's behaviour began to develop some erratic tendencies (wandering out of the house at all hours, cleaning out the refrigerator at midnight, defecating in inappropriate places) that Bonnie realized she would not be able to continue much longer in her role as a caregiver.

Booker roamed whenever the opportunity presented itself. Several times, he was kindly returned home by the neighbours, and once by the police who responded to a call and found him trying to get into the elementary school on a Sunday. Booker also developed a habit of stashing objects. Bonnie found odd things in odd places, like the post office keys in a box of light bulbs in the closet and his old age pension cheque in the cupboard under the plates. Once, she came across a deck of cards in the brown sugar container. As Booker couldn't remember where he had hidden things, he was constantly searching, although if Bonnie asked what he is looking for he couldn't tell her. *Oh, that thing,* he would say. *You know.*

Booker became fearful of being left alone. He followed Bonnie from room to room, even waited outside the bathroom when she was in there, asking every few minutes when she was coming out. He couldn't remember whether he had eaten or whether he had just been for a walk or even the names of his family members.

But Booker somehow remembered many things from the past. Once in a while the thickening cloud pulled back and a ray of memory or understanding flickered. He still enjoyed life such as it was—in the moment.

Bonnie knew when the time came. She and Randy made the rounds of several of Winnipeg's personal care homes and they settled on Belle Vista Lodge, a relatively new establishment close to their home. Booker was evaluated and approved for residency.

That was when Bonnie and Randy decided to take Booker on one last trip. They knew it would be his last. Bonnie made plans to retrace the travels of their honeymoon to Niagara Falls, over fifty years earlier.

chapter 28
Belle Vista Lodge

Belle Vista Lodge was a beautiful modern facility. All the rooms had wide bright windows overlooking a tastefully-landscaped courtyard. Bonnie and Randy were hugely impressed with their tour of Belle Vista. The white-covered tables in the dining room glowed with their fresh floral centrepieces and dark green place-mats; the airy common lounge had two televisions and a roomy kitchen area; flowering plants flourished at every window—everything spoke of tender loving care.

Booker's room was at the far end of the hallway. He was allowed to have his own television and this pleased him greatly, although most of the time he had no idea what he was watching. He had a roommate, a feeble man by the name of Theo Hryciuk who spoke only Ukrainian, and Bonnie was disappointed Booker would not have someone to talk to. This made the television all the more important, she believed.

Booker's wing was populated by seniors who were physically mobile but virtually everyone had some degree of dementia; the only exceptions were two women whose rooms were at the end of the hallway closest to the common lounge.

The day Dr. Booker Johnson arrived, the nursing staff swarmed him with attention. Bonnie and Randy left Belle Vista Lodge with a feeling of vast relief. Booker would be well cared for.

Booker's first introduction to life at Belle Vista Lodge was a trip to the dining room. It was not, however, the tastefully appointed dining room shown to Bonnie and Randy during their earlier tour. This room was beigely colourless and austere. There were no table cloths or napkins—just paper placemats and napkins in dispensers. Bonnie found out later that dementia patients were not admitted to the formal main dining room.

It was a blessing that Booker's senses of taste and smell were diminished. His first meal consisted of instant mashed potatoes, canned creamed corn and a flat piece of rubbery chicken with some kind of bland white sauce. There was orange jelly for dessert. Booker's appetite was still good and he ate everything.

Booker's immobile roommate Theo was hand-fed from a tray next to his bed. When Booker was returned to his room after dinner, Theo was lying bottom-naked on a rubber-backed pad on the bed. He had defecated on the pad. The attendant that was with Booker scolded Theo, who didn't appear to understand what he had done. The attendant left Theo without attending to the mess.

Booker sat in his chair, puzzled by the television remote in his hand. It was not at all like his remote at home and the configuration of buttons was absolutely foreign.

He put his hand into the pocket of his navy cardigan and pulled out a wrinkled scrap of paper. He tried to remember why it should be important. He smoothed the paper as much as he could and placed it in the drawer of his bedside table, far in at the back. It would be safe there.

chapter 29
Cloudy Sky

A thin white wisp of cloud wafted innocuously past the sun and cast a tiny unnoticed shadow on the earth. A few more wisps gathered and drifted, some melding together to form larger tufts of fluff. The fleeting shadows passed below, still mostly unseen. The wisps and tufts continued to join and multiply and raced in front of the sun and created ever-widening tracts of shade. The winds blew in puffs and gusts. The sky filled with darkening clouds, heavy and grey.

This was Dr. Booker Johnson's sky. He could no longer see past or through the clouds that veiled his consciousness. He couldn't remember the brilliant blue of the heavens or the beauty of a double rainbow, or make sense of the names or faces of once-familiar dear ones. His alzheimeric existence was marked by a monotonous day-to-day void of thought.

There were rare occasions when a tiny opening tore itself into the grey cloud shrouding Booker's mind, and he was allowed a fleeting glimpse of the past. Those openings might be ten seconds or half a minute or five minutes, who could say? The flashes usually occurred just when Booker was waking up and seemed to be part of an escaping dream, but in those moments he was fully and wonderfully aware that he was remembering.

The clarity of these glimpses was perfect and stunning, but ephemeral. If someone happened to be with Booker when the veil pulled back, he overflowed with excitement at his memory.

It would have been wonderful if Booker's recollections were more varied, but he was singularly fixated on a memory of a little girl he called Nellie. *She needs my help,* he would say over and over. *I have the name.* He would become animated and desperate to be understood. *She needs my help.*

On several occasions, Booker's pestering for help with Nellie became so insistent that the head nurse ordered medication to calm him. That worked well, and became standard procedure.

The rest of the staff at Belle Vista Lodge was uniformly disinterested and they consistently responded to his animated accounts by dismissing them as a dream or by simply changing the subject or by ignoring him altogether.

Booker's wife Bonnie witnessed half a dozen "memory snaps," as she called them, and Booker's son Randy saw two. Bonnie and Randy dismissed the obsession with "Nellie" as baseless. *There was never anyone in our family called Nellie*, they insisted. *We never knew anyone by that name.*

Both Randy and Bonnie were certain that a tiny part of Booker's mind still stored valid information—he had articulated tidbits to them during the memory incidents. He had asked meaningful questions. He seemed at times to understand their conversations, knew their names, and was aware of their relationships. Then, abruptly, the aperture in Booker's fog would pull itself shut.

Bonnie and Randy saw great hope in these little flashes of recall. They believed that the ravages of memory loss would someday be reversed, that the brain could still harbor in its con-voluted folds the capacity to organize and classify and commu-nicate. Bonnie was convinced that intense tactile stimulation was the key to recovery and she surrounded Booker with artifacts from his past—photographs of rafting and skiing and travel, his oil paintings and favourite books, his black leather gloves, an old woodworking catalogue—all carefully chosen to evoke memory. Randy added to the mix with a headset so Booker could listen to his beloved bagpipe music and Frank Mills' piano. Booker wasn't capable of operating the little CD player by himself so Bonnie enlisted the help of the nursing home staff to help him set up the very elementary little system. They always promised to do so, but Bonnie doubted they had ever even looked at it. And when she asked Booker, he just smiled and nodded.

Bonnie and Randy discussed their theories in depth with Booker's doctor, who nodded and smiled sympathetically but offered no validation to their belief that the Alzheimer-damaged mind might someday learn to re-invent itself.

Whenever Bonnie and Randy visited, Belle Vista Lodge was by all appearances an idyllic place. They had no way of knowing that when they said goodbye to Booker it reverted to its true nature, which was largely one of apathy and impatience.

Dr. Booker Johnson got no special recognition or treatment here. No one paid any attention to his occasional mention of a little girl who needed help.

Part Three

chapter 30
Jamie Howell

RCMP Corporal Jamie Howell squares his shoulders and nudges the front doorbell with his thumb, as if he is trying to gently poke it awake. Through the glass-paned door he hears bell chimes looping the first few bars of *Pop Goes the Weasel*. Over the past year the doorbell has been reprogrammed with a different children's song on at least a monthly basis. *Twinkle, Old MacDonald, Frere Jacques*. In August, it pealed *Happy Birthday*, and at Christmas time, *Away in a Manger*.

The door edges open a crack and Janelle St. Clair's eyes appear above the security chain. "Hey, Jamie. How's everything going?" She slips the bolt on the chain.

"I just finished my shift. Thought I'd drop by for a couple of minutes."

"Good timing. I just made some tea."

Howell steps in and bends over to remove his boots.

"Never mind the boots," she says. "Come on in."

Janelle leads the way to the kitchen. Howell slips into the closest chair. Janelle fills two china mugs. Tea should always be served in china, she insists. She holds the teapot high and allows the tea to cascade, splashing, into the cup. This improves the flavour by generating bubbles in the tea which re-oxygenate the water, she claims. Tea isn't Howell's first choice of beverage but he is learning to appreciate its therapeutic value. The many rituals of tea-making amuse Howell. He doesn't believe any of it, from the insistence on beginning with cold water to the heating of the teapot to the necessity of the tea cozy. But the end result is good, he has to admit. He agrees with Janelle, there is no other hot beverage that can quench thirst as effectively as tea.

The little air conditioner in the kitchen window convulses and rattles in its efforts to dispel the thick heat of the day. Janelle carries the mugs into the relative peace of the living room and Howell follows. She examines him, noting the spit-shine of his boots and his perfectly knotted tie.

"So. What's happening?"

It's the question he dreads. For far too long, there has been no answer. He buffs a fingerprint from the brim of his hat.

"I wish I had something new to tell you. We've been over all of it so many times…" He sets the hat between them on the sofa. "And now the file is being handed over to Dave Michales. I know Dave really well so I'll be able keep you updated on what's happening."

Corporal Howell isn't required to report to Janelle with updates. But he has been involved from the beginning of the investigation and as the months pass he is becoming increasingly obsessed with the case. He is convinced they have missed some little thing, some iota of information, perhaps a hunch or suspicion not yet articulated…a tiny key to the mystery.

Janelle shares this idea with conviction. For the past year she has been tearing away at her memory, peeling back layers and digging into dark corners. For her, this process is a relentless search for an elusive point in time and place. She returns to the same locus time and time again, always positive she has failed to notice some small and important clue, always coming up empty-handed.

"I'm driving down there again tomorrow," she says.

"I really wish you wouldn't."

"I have to. I go crazy if I'm not trying."

Corporal Howell has no jurisdiction over what Janelle St. Clair decides to do. The frequent trips to Kenora aren't unlawful. But they worry him.

"I have a few days off next month. I'd like to go down there with you." He looks at his gleaming boots. "You know, four eyes instead of two."

Janelle considers this for a few short seconds. "Really Jamie, I'm fine to go by myself. The road is good, my car is good, and I'll have my phone. The weather is supposed to be nice…"

Clearly frustrated, Howell runs his fingers through his blond hair. "It's none of that."

"Well, what, then? You're always trying to discourage me from going. You need to tell me why it's such a big deal."

Howell tips back his tea. "Most people don't realize all the things that can happen on a highway. Besides accidents and car trouble."

"Such as? It's time to clue me in."

He thinks carefully about how to frame his concerns without appearing to be over-protective.

"There's a huge population on the roads at any given time. It's like a massive cross-country city on the move, and everyone's anonymous. There's more crime on the highways than in any other place."

"There's crime everywhere, Jamie. What you're saying is like telling people they shouldn't go to Mexico for a holiday because some tourists got themselves killed down there. You just have to be careful. No matter where you go."

"There aren't any boundaries in effect out there, Janelle. There isn't any limit to criminal opportunity. Corruption, depravity, complete disregard for the law. The average person can't even imagine the things we know about. I could give you hundreds of examples of things that are happening on the highways. It's a dangerous place. "

"Honestly, Jamie, I think you're over-reacting. I've been over that stretch of road a dozen times and I've never felt even remotely threatened. Besides, it's only a couple of hours travel. Daylight hours. And I'm always back before dark. My God, you make me feel like a gullible grandmother who's going to get duped by a roadside scammer."

Corporal Howell drains his china mug and sets it on the table.

"At least the roadside scammers are visible. I know you'd know better than to stop. But it's the invisible operators you have to be aware of."

There is a small eye-roll that escapes his detection. "Give me the benefit of the doubt, Jamie. I know what to watch for." She pulls her feet up onto the sofa and draws her knees to her chest. "Besides, the most horrible thing that could happen to me has already happened. And it didn't happen on a highway."

There is no point in arguing with Janelle St. Clair; Howell learned that months ago. He checks his watch and reaches for his hat and shuffles his feet as if to get up. Janelle grabs his arm

"Wait, don't go yet. There's more tea. And I forgot to offer you some cookies."

Howell looks at his watch again. It is, after all, only seven. Cookies are non-existent in his apartment. He moves the shiny-peaked hat to the coffee table and loosens his tie.

MARGARET RIDDELL

Memory

All experience in life
takes place at the intersection of time and place.

The point of intersection is the present;
it is the juncture of here and now.
The locus of the present is fleeting;
like a dream, it cannot be touched.

The instant the point touches the grid,
it has already passed.
It is no longer here and now,
it is there and then.

Only in memory is it possible
to return to the intersection of the past.

M.R.

chapter 31
Kenora

Between Falcon Lake and Kenora, sections of the Trans-Canada Highway lie like a stiff grey carpet runner on the floor of a rock-walled corridor. Mosaics of names and cryptic aphorisms spread across the rocks like ugly gossip. People, probably highway employees, have splashed paint over the graffiti in some places. Sometimes the colour is almost close enough to the natural hues of the granite to be barely noticed, but more often than not it results in a glaring mismatched patchwork, often worse than the original defacement.

It's a Tuesday morning, hot already, the first week of July, and the air conditioner fan in the old blue Tempo is delivering a Sisyphean effort in its battle against the heat. Janelle looks for a safe place to stop for a few minutes for some fresh air.

The rock walls give way to a dark-watered pond on the side of the road and Janelle brakes gently, her right hand steadying the Little Mermaid backpack on the seat beside her. She checks her rear view mirror as an afterthought, and turns the Tempo onto the stony shoulder. The car crunches to a stop on the rough surface and she turns off the ignition and rolls down the windows to let a breeze pass through. She leans back on the headrest. Bobby Sperling perches in his usual place on top of the yellow backpack, up where he can see what is going on around him. She sets Bobby on the seat beside her and zips open the backpack and contemplates the clothing inside. *Will size six be too large? How much will Nellie have grown in a year? What do you think, Bobby Sperling?*

Bobby Sperling was discovered at a craft sale at the annual "Agate Hill Christmas Shopping Spree." He was the only red bear on the table. From the moment Nellie laid eyes on the plush animal, the shopping was over. Before they had time to detach the price tag from his fat little foot, she named him Bobby. He officially became Bobby Sperling a few days later, when Janelle explained to Nellie about his creators. They were a group of mostly older women from the tiny village of Sperling, and they had been making teddy bears for years. There was a time when Sperling was almost famous for the button-eyed bears. They were sold at craft sales and flea markets and Christmas events and they could even be ordered directly from the women who made them. They were special bears; they had arms and legs that swivelled independently. (These appendages were said to be held in place with old-fashioned pop bottle tops.)

Bobby Sperling went everywhere with Nellie—to day-care, shopping with Janelle, sleepovers at Auntie Zola-Rae's, the playground—and he always managed to be perched on the best vantage point she could find. He was even allowed in the bathroom where he viewed all proceedings from the top of the toilet tank. Not being washable, he was not allowed near the water. *Bears don't like baths, Mommy.*

Janelle steps onto the shoulder which is layered with fragments of dark grey crushed rock. A narrow stony rim borders the pond and eight Canada geese, a pair and six adolescent goslings, stand near the reeds at the edge of the water, their sharp black eyes locked on this intruder. On the other side of the highway the mottled grey of the vertical rock cut gives way to reddish granite. She locks the car and crosses the pavement to the base of the rock. It is as least thirty feet to the top but somehow people with their brushes and spray cans have managed to scale the nearly smooth face. She can see outlines of old graffiti shining through the new camouflage of paint, which is much too bright to blend with the ancient rock and hangs in long red drip-runs along its bottom edge. Might Nellie's name be printed in her baby script somewhere under the red paint? Would he or she or they have stopped here? Would they have allowed her to play for a minute on the strip of gravel along the pond, perhaps throw some sandwich leftovers or potato chips to the geese? No. They would have been in a hurry. And they wouldn't have wanted her to leave her name on the rocks.

Janelle leans against the hard wall. Though the morning is warm the rock is overnight-cold on her back. She tries to bring Nellie's face to mind but the image is hazy and dreamlike. The only face she can now truly visualize is the one in the photos she pulls from the backpack. She sees a beautiful child with long dark hair pulled into two ponytails and unruly wisps of angel-curl framing the lightly-freckled elfin face and clinging to the back of her neck. In the photo Nellie is wearing her favourite blue dress, the one with a slash of sparkles across the front. In every single picture, the love-worn red teddy bear Bobby Sperling is either in Nellie's arms or on her lap.

This is Janelle's fourth trip to Kenora since Nellie's abduction. There is solitude in the driving and it gives focus to her thoughts. Each time she has dissected the timeline meticulously, searching for the one elusive bit of information that will lead to her daughter's kidnappers. The recollections unfold in her consciousness like a repeating dream.

In the memory she is holding Nellie's hand. She traces their path from the parking lot to the Pavilion to the bandshell and then to the ice-cream stand and the face painters. Every detail is crystal-clear. Dread always overtakes her at the point where she is following Nellie through the crowd to the big orange and blue bouncy castle. The recollection ends while she is waiting at the bottom of the castle's exit slide. It was the last normal moment of Janelle's life.

Janelle crosses the highway back to the pond. The family of geese moves away down the gravelly shore as she approaches and she relaxes. She is afraid of the geese. Her grandparents always raised a small flock of them on their rocky farm in Manitoba's Interlake and one of the ganders—hissing, his neck stretched out, wings beating—had attacked Janelle when she was about five. The farm geese had no fear of humans, but Janelle suspects these wild birds might be more wary. Still, she is relieved when they swim into the reeds and away from the shore. There is something vaguely unsettling about the geese. It's not only the memory of her experience as a child, but a feeling that they are trying to tell her something.

She can see a narrow strip of sand close to the water's edge and she clambers down over the rock-piled embankment. Closer to the shore, goose manure dots the rocks. She picks her way to the sand which has been kept clean by a small constant lapping of sheltered wavelets. She sits on a hump-backed grey rock and traces letters with a twig in the flat sand at water's edge. NELLIE. A B C D E F G. 1 2 3 4 5 6.

Janelle closes her eyes and feels the hot sun beat down on her back. *I did this very same thing with Nellie.* The deja-vue slams into her like a gust of wind. *But when was that? Where were we?*

The geese waddle out of sight behind a patch of blackish reeds. Janelle scratches a wide heart in the coarse sand beside the letters. *Yes! I remember doing that, too.* She climbs back up over the rocks to the Tempo. She spreads the photos out on the seat of the car. They are covered with clear plastic to protect them from the wear of handling. Many strangers have looked at the faces of this child with her dark hair pulled up in an unruly topknot or in ponytails or just falling around her face. *Have you seen this little girl? Her hair color might have been changed. Or it could have been cut.* They all shake their heads. She puts the photos back in their folder and edges the car back onto the highway.

chapter 32
Last Known Whereabouts

Janelle drives into the parking lot at Aunt Maggie's Truck Stop. This is her fourth visit to Maggie's in the past year. She is always drawn to the table across from the last window booth. She orders coffee and the lunch special and shows the waitress the photos.

She's five and a half now, but she's small for her age. She called 911 from here a year ago. For the ten-thousandth time Janelle pictures Nellie's fingers working the emergency numbers on the rotary dial of the ancient pay phone.

Someone must have seen her here? Noticed something strange, something that didn't fit? The waitress shakes her head.

All leads have been checked, no stone left unturned. Everything possible has been done, the police have told her. The clichés of it all make her sick.

Someone has missed something. But even after all these months, Janelle is convinced there is still a sign to be found.

Janelle pushes her coffee cup away and gathers the photos. She rummages in her handbag for a couple of dollars to leave for the waitress and makes her way to the cash register near the door. Around the corner she can see the payphone, in full view of the counter. The payphone is an antique, kept by Aunt Maggie's Truck Stop because it was one of the first ever installed along the highway, way back when the restaurant was first built. Although it is operational, it is virtually never used, except by the odd tourist who wants to go back in time.

But Nellie used it.

The 911 operator tried to keep the child talking, as the recording showed, but the little voice stopped after a few seconds. The audio was faint and muffled, but everyone who heard and analyzed it agreed on one thing. The voice had said, "This is Nellie. I need help."

Aunt Maggie's Truck Stop was Nellie's last known whereabouts.

Janelle pays for her coffee and a copy of the local newspaper, the *Northern Shield*. She heads for the door, but is drawn back to the telephone. *The last known thing Nellie touched.* Janelle picks up the receiver and presses it against her face. Its hard cold blackness reminds her of the chill of the rock cut.

She goes outside, where heat ripples from the pavement of the parking lot. She realizes she forgot to leave the window of the Tempo down a little. It will be like a furnace inside. She opens the doors to let the slight breeze blow through and she sits, waiting for the car to cool a little, on one of the small grey boulders which is strategically placed to keep people from driving over the flowerbed. Scaled-down graffiti covers the rock. Brent was here. PAX. Mark Hoyes, Toronto. Les and Lynn, in a heart. A pentagram. Janelle shudders. The car is still hot but she slides into it anyway, letting the blistering vinyl burn the backs of her thighs through her jeans.

MARGARET RIDDELL

The breeze diminishes the heat in the car and Janelle browses through the *Northern Shield*. Not much of interest, she notes, just the usual stories of local interest. Page three, on the other hand, has been sensationalized. There are three stories: a murder conviction, a human interest angle, and a manslaughter case.

A man by the name of Jervis Oswald Strunk has just been found guilty in Kenora Court of multiple rapes and a murder. *What an ugly name.* Janelle wonders if there is any basis in fact for the theory that a person's name can have an influence on their behaviour. If there is, she supposes Jervis Oswald Strunk had a strike against him right from the beginning.

According to the newspaper, several victims had identified Strunk, including a local sixteen-year-old girl who had been viciously raped and beaten and was found unconscious in a campground washroom near the Minaki turn-off. Police had apparently stopped Strunk on a routine traffic check, and on the floor in the back of his car they found a handbag belonging to a missing Kenora woman, Erica Slesiuk. Mrs. Slesiuk's badly decomposed and wildlife-mauled remains were not found until weeks later at the bottom of a steep rock embankment along a side road, only a few miles from her home. Strunk admitted to the rape charges filed by the girl but vehemently denied he had anything to do with the murder. Traces of Erica Slesiuk's blood on the handbag proved otherwise, the jury decided.

Right below the story about Strunk's conviction is a more personal story, recounting Mike Slesiuk's reaction to the trial and detailing the events leading up to his wife's disappearance. There is a picture of the couple, smiling and happy, perhaps an anniversary photo.

The third article dealt with a vehicular manslaughter charge. A Manitoba trucker was found guilty of the deaths of two cyclists just west of Kenora. The incident happened around the same time as the murder and rape.

The stories have a common detail. The crimes took place on the same date: July 2—a date Janelle knows well. Nausea wells up in her throat. She must have passed the place where Erica Slesiuk's body was dumped and the campground where the badly beaten teenager was found. She must have driven past the place where the cyclists were killed. Nellie was here on that very day—the day she made her 911 call. Did she have contact with any of them? Could any of them have been in the restaurant when she was there?

The steady parade of traffic continues its unbroken stream past Aunt Maggie's Truck Stop. *Any of those vehicles could be carrying crazies. Right now.* What was it her Mountie friend Jamie Howell had told her? *At any given time the highway has a population of millions. Criminals use it as their place of business. It's one of the most dangerous places in the country.*

It had been difficult to appreciate his concern at the time. But now, she understands. He was right.

NORTHERN SHIELD

Strunk Found Guilty in Murder of Local Woman

Almost a year to the day since Erica Slesiuk of Kenora was murdered, Jervis Oswald Strunk has been convicted of the horrific crime.

The jury of seven men and five women returned a unanimous verdict of guilty after hearing three weeks of testimony and deliberating for only one hour.

MARGARET RIDDELL

Strunk's arrest in the case had followed a routine traffic stop for a minor infraction involving a broken tail light. Ontario Provincial Police discovered a blood-soaked handbag on the back seat of Strunk's car. The bag was identified as belonging to Erica Slesiuk, who had been missing for several days.

Throughout the trial, Strunk vehemently denied any involvement in Slesiuk's murder, but the jury decided otherwise. Bloodstains on the red purse found in the back seat of Strunk's car proved to be a match to Ms Slesiuk, and fingerprints on the purse were confirmed to be Strunk's.

Judge Henry Armstrong has set August 15 as the date for Strunk's sentencing.

In an earlier trial this spring, Strunk was convicted of the beating and rape of a local teenager, who recognized him in television coverage of his arraignment for Slesiuk's murder.

Victim's Husband Relieved at Conviction

"I can't believe it's finally over," said Mike Slesiuk yesterday after a jury found Jervis Strunk guilty of the murder of Slesiuk's wife Erica. "It's been a long year, waiting for justice. And now Erica can rest in peace."

His words summed up the feelings of many residents of the area.

A year ago, Slesiuk picked his wife up from work at Maggie's Truck Stop on the western outskirts of Kenora.

He drove back into town to drop her off at the Lakeland Mall to do some shopping, and they agreed to meet at the main door in two hours.

But Erica Slesiuk never showed up. She did not answer her cell phone. Mike Slesiuk waited for half an hour before assuming that his wife had taken a ride home with a friend, as she often did.

When Erica still had not returned home the following morning, Slesiuk filed a missing persons report. An intense search for the woman uncovered no clues as to her whereabouts.

A break in the investigation came a few days later when Jervis Strunk, a transient, was stopped for a minor vehicle infraction. His expired driver's licence led officers to search his car, where they found a bloodstained purse belonging to Ms Slesiuk.

The case against Strunk proceeded without a body until late September. A jogger running along a private access road east of Kenora followed his frantically distracted dog to the bottom of a steep rock embankment where he discovered the badly decomposed and wildlife-mauled remains of Ms Slesiuk.

Manitoba Trucker Guilty of Manslaughter

A Manitoba long-haul trucker was convicted last week of Unintentional Vehicular Manslaughter in the deaths of two cyclists last year near Kenora.

Katie Maybank of Halifax, Nova Scotia and John Lindblom of Brandon were completing a cross-country cycling trip that had begun in Halifax six weeks earlier. They set out for the last leg of their journey from Kenora to Winnipeg on July 2. The two were run down west of Kenora when they stopped at the side of the highway for an undetermined reason.

Finn Erikson of Winnipeg was "grossly impaired," said prosecutor Andrew Barth. The trucker had deliberately falsified his trucker's log and was estimated to have been driving for nearly twenty-two hours without any significant stops for rest, the jury was told. Toxicology tests showed high levels of stimulants in Erikson's system, Barth said.

Erikson's Driver's Licence was revoked immediately after the accident and his truck was seized by investigators.

In a separate indictment, Erikson was charged and found guilty of smuggling tobacco when hundreds of contraband packages were discovered in hidden compartments in his truck.

chapter 33
Return Trip

Janelle puts the *Northern Shield* on the passenger seat and starts the car. She takes one last look at Aunt Maggie's Truck Stop. She can still feel the chill of the telephone receiver on her cheek. She leaves the car windows down for some air and enters the highway, her right hand on the yellow backpack.

Fifteen minutes of travel brings her back to the small dark pond along the highway where she stopped earlier. She drives past the spot, makes a U-turn on the highway and parks on the stony shoulder beside the pond. The Canada geese are still there, now sunning themselves on the thin strip of sand, right on top of Janelle's alphabet scratchings. One of the birds, the large gander, has chosen to relax in the centre of the outline of the heart. Janelle leaves the car and stands at the top of the embankment, waving her arms to scare the geese away from the letters. The gander pulls himself to his full height and flaps his huge wingspan of nearly two meters. He stretches his neck and pumps his head up and down and his warning hiss sounds like water sizzling on a grill. Janelle manages to scramble back to the car just as he launches his attack. Her mind goes back to the incident with the cranky geese owned by her grandparents and she involuntarily touches the long scar on her arm. She had been lucky then—her grandfather was only a few feet away and pulled the enraged bird from her back. She was lucky today too—there would have been no rescuer if the huge bird had managed to sink his small but sharp talons into her back and beat violently with his hard-feathered wings.

She closes her eyes and leans back against the headrest, sweating profusely. She smells the memory of the summer breeze, sees a duck pond, hears the angry sizzle of hissing Canada Geese, and is aware of people—a seedy-looking man nearby and a friendly young couple further down the edge of the pond. The earlier deja-vue comes into focus and Janelle knows it is part of the memory. She struggles to understand the connection. A duck pond comes into focus; not the pond at the bottom of the embankment, but a more formal pond, shaded by willows and bordered by a walkway.

Assiniboine Park is one of Winnipeg's oldest and most beloved green spaces, wide and open and safe, the perfect place for families. Its eleven hundred landscaped acres stretch the length of the aspen-oak Assiniboine Forest to the south, and embrace the wide and lazy Assiniboine River on the north.

And now, the park has decided to unfold its recollections.

The visit to the park that day had been a consolation outing of sorts. Janelle had three weeks' vacation coming in August and planned to take Nellie to Canada's Wonderland Park north of Toronto. Nellie would celebrate her fifth birthday while they were there. It would have been Nellie's first major holiday and her first airplane ride. The two of them spent hours poring over the brochures and maps and schedules. Nellie had the carte-blanche privilege of picking out the rides she wanted to go on and the events she wanted to take part in. Janelle booked tickets, ride vouchers, and reservations.

But Nellie's excitement was out of control and Janelle wished she had waited a little longer to tell her about the holiday. She looked for a distraction, and the Canada Day Celebrations at Assiniboine Park fit the criteria perfectly. They decided to visit as many attractions as possible before attending the outdoor stage celebrations.

Janelle rests her head on the steering wheel and closes her eyes. She can hear the blood-swishing of her heartbeat in her ears. The memories awaken and burgeon into full bloom, growing and spreading in intricate detail.

The Starting Point

One must get hold of a starting point.

*It often happens that, though a person cannot recollect at the moment,
yet by seeking he can do so, and discovers what he seeks.*

*One who recollects will be able, somehow, to move,
solely by his own effort,
to the term next to the starting point.*

*…From the starting point…the mind receives an impulse to move
sometimes in the required direction, and at other times otherwise…*

*…One may be mistaken, and think that he remembers
when he really does not.*

The art of recollecting differs from that of remembering.

*Recollection is the reinstatement in consciousness
of some thing that was there before but had disappeared.*

*The Basic Works of Aristotle.
(Ed Richard McKeon)
Modern Library; New edition 2001*

chapter 34
Clarity

For the first time in a year Janelle is able to trace the path she
and Nellie took that morning.

The duck pond is first on the agenda. Janelle parks her blue
Tempo in the zoo lot and they gather their backpacks and water.
The pond is a short walk across a grassy area. Bobby Sperling,
Nellie's red teddy bear, sits in the open top of Nellie's backpack
so he will be able to see. Nellie never goes anywhere without
Bobby Sperling.

A family of Mallard ducks lazes in the morning sun in the
shallow area next to the pathway, the half-grown ducklings in
a tight semi-circle around their parents. A pair of wood ducks
cruises under the shade of a large willow. *Look, Mommy! Someone
put beautiful paint on one of them!* Janelle explains that the male
duck is lucky to have such handsome colours. *Does his wife want
nice colours too? No sweetie, I think she's happy with her own feathers.*

A gaggle of Canada Geese approaches an old man standing
along the shoreline of the pond. It's a hot day, but he is dressed
in dark sweats and a dirty green hoodie. He appears to have
a bag of goose food, and the birds know it. Janelle is nervous
of the large birds and she and Nellie approach cautiously. *Can*

we feed them some of our lunch, Mommy? I don't think so, sweetie. People food isn't healthy for them. The man moves toward Nellie and offers a handful of brown pellets. Close up, Janelle can see he is not old at all, but he is unshaven and the proffered hand is dirty with something dark like oil. Janelle grabs Nellie's hand and pulls her away. *Sorry, we were just leaving.*

They turn away and head past the man around the north end of the pond. One of the geese follows them looking for a handout and Janelle shoos it away, but this is enough to make the goose defensive and it stretches out its neck and bobs its handsome head up and down and hisses a warning. Janelle stiffens. Nellie laughs fearlessly at the sound and the goose spreads its wings and continues its approach.

A young man comes running from somewhere, waving his arms and yelling, and the goose decides to back off. A woman, probably his wife, follows him around the pond. Thank you, Janelle calls. They turn back and smile.

The seedy-looking man is watching with interest. "See?" he says. "If you'da took some food to give him he would'a left you alone."

Janelle and Nellie backtrack across the parking lot and enter the zoo. The first stop is the bear enclosure where two polar bears are taking turns cooling off in a small pool of water. One of the bears gets bored and dives into a deeper moat-like pond. Nellie thinks this is hilarious. They move on to the big cats— tigers, lions, snow leopards—but none of the animals are interested in movement. It's too hot and they sprawl in the shade, blinking an occasional lazy eye. A pathway through the trees leads to the camel enclosure, where there is a small play area. Nellie drags Bobby Sperling up the ladder on a camel statue and slides down a chute into the sand. Janelle snaps a picture with her little pocket camera. The fenced pen nearby boasts several different types of camels, all of them crankily dragging matted sheds of hair. They watch the passing people with supercilious stares.

It's too far to walk to the Tropical House, so Janelle and Nellie backtrack to the monkey cages. Unlike the big cats, the monkeys are enjoying the heat and performing wild antics for the crowd. Nellie holds Bobby Sperling as close to the cage as she can reach and one of the monkeys pokes out a paw, almost close enough to grab the bear.

A young couple stands beside Nellie, laughing at the simian sideshow. Janelle studies them. They look familiar. The man is very tall, well over six feet, slim but muscular, his well-tanned face framed by light blond hair. He is dressed in khaki cargo shorts and a red golf shirt. His wife (at least Janelle assumes she is his wife) is very attractive with a tiny upturned nose, deep blue eyes, and long dark hair. She is wearing a bright yellow sundress. The man bends toward Nellie. "You should stand back a bit, honey. You never know what monkeys might do."

He turns to Janelle. "Didn't we just see you at the duck pond?"

She laughs in recognition. "Yes, you did. You saved Nellie from the goose!"

The man smiles at Nellie. "Take care, little lady."

Janelle would like to stop for lunch but Nellie wants to go to the place where they have "the funny little animals that stand up." She means the meerkats. They make a beeline for the Kinsmen Discovery Centre. Nellie takes Bobby Sperling out of the backpack so he can have a closer view of everything. Just ahead, Janelle catches another glimpse of the woman in the yellow sundress. A doorway leads to the Farmyard Barn, but

Nellie decides to bypass it in favour of the souvenir shop on the way out of the zoo, where Janelle allows her to pick out a book about monkeys and a blue butterfly night light.

They cross back through the zoo parking lot to the playground area. Janelle stops at the car on the way by to pick up her backpack and a blanket. In the playground Nellie gravitates to a large sandbox. Janelle smooths the sand in the box and Nellie prints and draws stick figures with her finger. She can already form most of the letters, and all the numbers up to 10. Showing off, she scratches out "ABCDEFG, 123456. *It needs a fence around it, Mommy.* " Janelle draws a huge heart around the masterpiece.

Janelle spreads the denim picnic blanket on the grass near the swings. Nellie pulls the backpack in front of her and begins her ritual exploration. Everything comes out—wrapped sandwiches, grape juice boxes, a bag of homemade peanut butter cookies, 60 SPF sunscreen, mosquito spray, colouring book and crayons, a new novel by Nicholas Sparks for Janelle, and a one-liter bottle of water. Nellie digs out Janelle's wallet from the bottom of the backpack. She insists on looking at the pictures inside, especially those of her father Patrick, whom she had never known. She never tires of hearing Janelle tell her about how much he would have loved his baby girl.

Nellie sets out blue napkins and props Bobby Sperling against her Little Mermaid backpack. *He should eat first, Mommy. He's really hungry from all this walking.*

Janelle organizes the lunch while Nellie fusses with Bobby Sperling. When the bear is settled, she reaches into the kangaroo pocket on the front of her blue T-shirt and extracts her own treasure, a red vinyl wallet with white and yellow daisies embossed on one side. The wallet was a spur of the moment gift from Auntie Zola-Rae.

"Do you want to see the pictures of all my children?" she asks Janelle.

Janelle pretends enthusiasm, though she has seen the pictures dozens of times. They are just ragged cutouts of dolls from the Sears Wish Book inserted painstakingly in the plastic photo compartments.

"And this is my secret compartment," Nellie says. She always shows this as if she is revealing an enormous secret. She opens the billfold side of the wallet and looks furtively from side to side, then lifts a flap of vinyl, like a con artist opening his coat to show his array of watches for sale.

"Why isn't there anything in there?" Janelle asks.

"I'm saving it for something really important."

"And what kind of thing would be important enough to put in there?"

Nellie deliberates with mock seriousness. "Well, I could put my house and phone number in there in case I get lost. Or if something bad happened and I had to tell you a message I would write it down and put it under there.

Janelle goes along with the scenario. "What kind of message would you tell me?"

"Well," Nellie intones importantly, "I would put a phone number. Or I would put a picture of somebody. Or the name of a car."

"Like our Tempo, or Grandpa's Pontiac?" Janelle smiles at the absurdity of a four-year-old thinking she can differentiate between makes of cars, let alone write the information down.

"No, Mommy, don't be silly," Nellie answers in exaggerated indignation. "Like the name on the back of a car. You know, the numbers."

This is not something they have ever talked about. Nellie is clever; of that there is no doubt.

They had, however, talked about how children had to be very careful. Not to speak with people who were not friends. Not to approach an unknown car. Not to take candy or gifts. Not even to help a stranger look for a poor sad lost puppy.

They eat lunch. Nellie splashes grape drink on the blanket when she tries to insert the straw in the box. *Bobby Sperling doesn't like the pickles in the ham sandwich, Mommy. Is it okay if he just has cookies?*

Janelle notices a cluster of picnic tables on the other side of the swings. A young couple sits at one of the tables. Janelle recognizes them from the duck pond and the monkey cages. The dark-haired woman in the yellow dress appears to be crying, and the man in the red shirt is consoling her.

There is only one thing left to do before they go to the Canada Day Celebrations on the other side of the park. This is always the highlight of Nellie's day—a ride on the little steam train. They climb onto a car near the engine and sit in a front-facing seat. Just as the train whistles its departure, a man clambers into a seat one car ahead of them, facing Janelle and Nellie. It's the strange man from the duck pond. A thick stench of tobacco smoke emanates from him and wafts backward into the train as the cars move out. Janelle draws Nellie close. *It's all right, sweetie. You're perfectly safe.* They switch seats so they can face away from him. The trip seems to take longer than usual and by the time they disembark the smelly disheveled man has disappeared. Ahead in the crowd are the man with the red shirt and the woman in the yellow sundress.

It's time to go to the Canada Day Celebration. Janelle's feet are burning and she feels what might be the beginning of a blister. She in anxious to get back to the car because she wants to move it to a parking lot closer to the festivities. In the parking lot three obnoxious teen boys hover near the Tempo, spouting obscenities for the benefit of anyone in earshot. One of them leans on the hood.

"Hey, lady ho, give us a ride!"

"Yeah, I bet you know how to give a good ride!"

They roar with guttural laughter. "Hey, how about the kid?"

Janelle shakes as she tries to work the key into the doorlock. The boys come closer. She knows their threatening demeanor is just that—demeanor. Still, it makes her more than a little uneasy.

A loud voice thunders behind Janelle. "Get the hell out of here, creeps."

It's the man in the red golf shirt. This strikes Janelle as a major co-incidence.

"Are you all right?" he asks.

Janelle nods. "Thank you."

"Don't mention it."

His red Subaru is parked right beside her. He opens the passenger door for his companion in the yellow sundress. He backs out slowly and rolls down his window as they pass. "You going to be ok?"

Janelle watches the three boys swagger across the parking lot. "Yes, we'll be fine. Thanks again."

She is glad to be out of the zoo lot and on the way to the parking area near the Conservatory.

Oh, my God. The Conservatory parking lot. That's where I've been starting from all this time. But that's not where it started.

This picture-perfect recall of the morning at the park has shaken her. *How could I have forgotten the first half of the day?*

Janelle rolls down the window of the Tempo. Beads of perspiration shine on her forehead. The angry goose has long since gone back to the pond.

She is convinced that her newly-awakened recollection holds the answer to Nellie's disappearance. She will beat the memory to death to find it. But for now, it's time to go home.

A few miles west of Kenora Janelle passes over one of the many long rises in the road. Late day sunlight refracts off specks of mica in the rose-colored granite of the Canadian Shield, and the ditches on both sides are wild with tiny daisies and bluebells and black-eyed Susans. She stops the Tempo and gets out and picks her way through the scattered stones and boulders in the ditch. She gathers a spray of flowers from the profusion of colour before her.

A pair of white crosses pokes up from a clutter of rock nearby. She can make out the names "John" and "Katie" on the crosses, and a date, July 2, last year. Janelle lowers herself to a small boulder and sits facing the markers. She knows they mark the site of the accident where the trucker killed the cyclists. The flowers, squeezed and hot in her fist, begin to wilt, a dull cast transforming their petals. Traffic flows over the rise in the road and the vehicle sounds wax and wane like passing screams.

After a long time, Janelle stands and approaches the crosses. She arranges the limp spray of flowers between them. She returns to her car, which is once again an inferno inside, but she gets in anyway and pulls back on to the road. She doesn't look back at the white markers or the rock where she sat. Wedged tightly against the base of the boulder is a red vinyl wallet, nearly invisible, its white and yellow daisies dulled and darkened beneath the dust.

MARGARET RIDDELL

Janelle arrives back in Winnipeg just after sunset. She gathers her collection of pictures and Nellie's backpack from the car. Bobby Sperling is still peering out from the unzipped top. The day's events have exhausted her, but in a positive way. She can't wait to tell Jamie Howell about her new recollections.

but·ter·fly ef·fect *definition, noun*

*the phenomenon whereby a minute localized change
in a complex system can have large effects elsewhere.*

*The term was originally coined in reference
to atmospheric science. It has been said that
the tiny air currents from the flutter of a butterfly's wings
could set off a chain reaction that might have the potential
to cause a hurricane in another part of the world.*

*The term "butterfly effect" is often also applied
to human behaviour and is often used to describe
how a seemingly small and random event
can have far-reaching implications in the future.
Something as simple as a bus ticket...*

chapter 35
Evertons

It's a one-way bus ticket from Blackburn Harbour to Saskatoon.

They are furious when she tells them. *After everything we've done for you, you're just going to up and leave? You could show a bit of gratitude. You can't walk away from here, just like that. Who'll help your mom in the craft shop? You'll never be able to make it on your own out there.*

But Art and Molly McMillan cannot stop Denita from going and they refuse to help her. The next morning she walks down to the Blackburn Harbour Café to catch the bus to the Port-aux-Basques Ferry, lugging the scarred black suitcase that had once belonged to her Great-Aunt Dodie. Her two younger brothers follow along, wishing they were going with her and knowing that someday they will follow. Denita can see them waving as the ferry eases out into the Gulf of St. Lawrence. She knows she will never be back.

The trip takes several days and Denita is thoroughly bus-weary by the time the Greyhound delivers her to downtown Saskatoon. She uses most of her remaining cash to rent a small economy car and she buys a city map to locate Marcy's address.

Marcy White had been Denita's best friend back in Blackburn Harbour and she had been relentless in persuading Denita to "get off the rock." *There are lots of jobs in Saskatoon,* she wrote, *I'll help you find something. Anything will be better than back there. You can stay with me, I have space.*

Saskatoon's late-day traffic is overwhelming. Stop lights half a block ahead, left lane merging, bumper to bumper, siren coming up from behind, a driver gesturing obscenely—Denita glances at him momentarily—and looks back in time to realize she is going to rear-end the small car in front of her.

The young man is irate at first. He directs her to follow him and they pull onto a side street and get out to inspect the damage. The rental car has sustained a slightly bent licence plate and the young man's car shows no visible damage.

"We'd better exchange information, just in case," he says. "Do you have anything to write on?"

Denita finds a pocket calendar in her handbag and tears out the January page and writes her name and Marcy's address and telephone number on it. She tears out the February page and hands it to him and he prints on it carefully and they exchange the papers.

He tries to sound serious. "Better watch where you're going, Ok?"

He folds his lanky frame back into his sub-compact and eases back onto the main thoroughfare. Denita sits in her car and examines the February page.

Danny Everton. A telephone number. That is all. And the only thing she remembers noticing about him is that he was very tall.

Marcy thinks the whole thing is hilarious. *Saskatoon drivers,* she says. *You've gotta love them. Don't worry about it, Denita.*

She establishes Denita in a corner of the living room of her tiny apartment and they sit up with a magnum of wine until two in the morning talking and giggling, just like they used to do back in Blackburn Harbour.

Marcy drags herself off to work the next day at the GrowGreen Garden Centre and leaves Denita to recuperate. Marcy has a day off coming to her and she promises to use it to take Denita job-hunting on Thursday. Then they will go out for dinner, Marcy's treat.

Marcy is right about the job market in Saskatoon. One of GrowGreen's affiliates is looking for help in their propagation department, and they hire Denita on the spot.

That night Denita and Marcy take a bus to the Riverside Café for dinner. The hostess settles them by a window overlooking the wide South Saskatchewan River. Denita is admiring the downstream view of the multiple arched University Bridge when a voice asks if they want to order drinks. She looks up at the very tall waiter and feels the red flowing into her cheeks. It is Danny Everton, he of the rear-ended car.

He is as professional as a waiter can be—attentive, helpful, and perhaps a little friendlier than necessary, but he makes no reference to their earlier meeting.

A week later he calls Denita at Marcy's. They go out to a movie at the old Roxy Theatre and have soft ice cream at the DairiWip and walk along the river pathway above the South Saskatchewan.

The two of them have a lot in common. Danny had become estranged from his parents in North Battleford when he refused to have any part of the family's construction business. He hoped they would eventually be able to reconcile, but a drunk driver killed them on the highway to Lloydminster before Danny had a chance to restore the family dynamic. The Evertons left everything to Danny's older brother Marty, and the estrangement seems to be irreversible.

Danny, unable to find a direction in his life, works part time for a hardware store during the day and at the Riverside Café most evenings. He has a small apartment overlooking the river, not far from the restaurant. It's big enough for the two of them, he says, and Denita agrees. She moves in after their fourth date.

By the end of the summer Denita is pregnant and this turn of events provides Danny with the focus he needs, but it proves to be a challenge to find a job that will enable him to support his family. He continues his part-time job at the hardware and works for a short time in Sears but the promised hours do not materialize.

Out of desperation he accepts a position as a restaurant manager at the seedy old Westridge Hotel. The Westridge had been a classy place in its day. Danny is determined to restore some of that glory, and the restaurant seems like a good place to start.

By the time little Evan is born the following spring, the Westridge has undergone a massive cleanup. The restaurant is busy, rooms are being booked, modest events have begun to reserve meeting rooms, and Danny Everton is promoted to the job of manager.

Danny and Denita get married in a civil ceremony at the City Hall and find a tiny two-story house in Riversdale. Denita sends her parents a letter announcing both the birth and the wedding. Her mother responds with a telephone call of measured congratulations.

Little Evan is a firecracker. He learns to walk before he is ten months old but Denita still puts him in a wheeled walker for much of the time as he has absolutely no judgment as to where he should and should not go. When he is just over a year old, Evan tumbles down the basement stairs in the walker. He fractures both arms and needs stitches on his knee. A few months later he falls out of his high chair as the restraining strap comes undone when he tries to reach something on the kitchen table. He cuts his forehead on the edge of the table and again needs stitches.

The overzealous doctor at the clinic reports what he calls "a situation" to Family Services, who send case workers to inspect the home and to "educate" Denita.

And then Evan is found unconscious in his crib with a blanket tangled around his neck. Denita calls an ambulance and Danny meets them at the hospital but it is too late. Because of the frequency and seriousness of Evan's accidents, an inquest is called. Denita and Danny are eventually exonerated of allegations of neglect and abuse.

The Westridge Hotel continues its climb back to respectability. Best Western buys the hotel and renames it The Westridge Heights Inn. Along with massive room and restaurant renovations, they add an indoor pool and waterslide to the facility. In the space of three years, the Westridge has morphed from a shabby hotel to a desirable downtown destination. It is all because of Danny Everton.

Denita is back at GrowGreen Nurseries and works on the front lines with the landscape architects who buy their materials there. She takes a correspondence course in Landscape Design and her creative work is sought after by new home builders—so much so that she establishes her own design company, Signature Terrace.

Emily Rose Everton is born three years after Evan's death. Family Services resurfaces and lurks ominously in the background, waiting for a reason to interfere. They never get a chance. Emily is a precocious and daring child, but Denita hovers relentlessly. There will be no more incidents. The Evertons upgrade to a suburban home in the southern part of the city.

Emily is almost five when Danny is offered a position as manager of a prestigious new hotel in Winnipeg, the Colonnade Resort and Spa. It is an opportunity too good to pass up. They have a month to prepare for the move, and Denita makes arrangements to move Signature Terrace along with them.

chapter 36
Moving Day

Alec and Moira Tanner, still in their pyjamas and in their usual perpetual mood of nosiness, are draped over the white good-neighbour fence that separates their property from the Everton's yard.

"Sure a hell of a storm last night, eh?" Alec calls to Danny.

"Yep, think we got over ten centimeters, according to the rain gauge," says Danny.

"So, all packed and ready to go?"

"Hope so. Denita's done a fantastic job of getting everything together. Now all we have to do is get it all unpacked when we get there."

"That's a big job. I remember when we moved here, it was over two months before we got everything squared away. Still some things we never found, and that was six years ago. "

Moira Tanner opens the two-way gate between their yards and walks over to where the Norsask Logistics moving vans are parked. Alec follows her.

"So, Denita, you must be really really excited?" Moira asks. "How about Emily? Is she looking forward to be moving?"

Denita hesitates and glances at Danny. He takes the question.

"Well, she's a little young to really understand what's going on. But yes, she's happy that she's going to have a duck pond at the new house. And there's a little playhouse in the back yard. I think she's more thrilled about that than anything."

"Where is she, anyway? I would've thought she'd be right out here in the middle of things."

"We thought it would be better if she stayed with her grandmother over in Asherville for a couple of days," Danny says. "You know Emily. She has a tendency to get into things, and it's been pretty hectic around here."

"I didn't know you had family in Asherville." Moira quizzes. "Is that your parents, Denita?"

"No, It's my mom," Danny says quickly. "She's going to bring Emily down to Winnipeg next week, after we get unpacked and settled."

"Oh, darn, that's too bad she's not here," says Moira. "We're really going to miss her with all her funny little antics. She's always been our favourite little neighbour girl, you know. And now we won't get to see her before she goes. And I even made some Smartie cookies for her to take to eat along the way. But I guess I can still give them to you, would that be all right? They'll keep for a few days." Moira comes up for air. "Will you tell her goodbye for us?"

Danny gives Moira a friendly pat on the back. "We sure will, Moira. Emily always loved running over to your place for a visit."

"Oh, I know she did. And we'll really miss that. Of course, we'll miss you guys, too. I sure hope the people that are moving into your house will be good neighbours. You just never know, do you?"

She moves close to give Denita a hug. "Are you ok, Denita? You look exhausted, with those dark rings under your eyes."

Denita is stiff in the hug. She nods her head and forces a smile.

Alec finally gets another chance to speak. "Well, it looks like the crew is ready to start loading, Danny. We'd better let you two get back to the job at hand. Take care, now."

"Yes, we'll let you get to it," Moira agrees. "But I'll bring the cookies over before you go. Don't want you to leave without them!"

She and Alec head back to the gate in the fence.

"Oh, I just remembered," Moira calls back. "I need to get your address in case we come down there for a visit. I have an aunt in Winnipeg, you know, my mother's side. It's been ages since I've seen her, but now that you're going to be there too, well, I could kill two birds with one stone. Right, Alec?"

Long after the gate in the fence draws shut, Moira's exasperating cheerfulness echoes into the dark cave of the garage.

Finally the Norsask Logistics moving crew gets busy.

It is after seven that evening when Danny and Denita arrive in Winnipeg. They have complimentary rooms for two nights at the Colonnade Resort and Spa right downtown. That will give Norsask Logistics time to complete the relocation to the gated community of Willow Bluff just north of the city.

Denita hasn't spoken all the way from Saskatoon. She has not said a word since the accident. Danny decides not to pressure her to talk about it. Not yet.

The two-storey house at Willow Bluff overlooks a small retention pond. A gingerbread-style playhouse nestles between the house and the pond. The previous owners have left a wooden play structure on the premises, and a tiny arched bridge spans a dry-creek flower garden. The place is a child's dream come true.

Denita unpacks the boxes that the movers left in what was to have been Emily's room. She makes the bed with Emily's favourite Disney Princess bedding and arranges a dozen stick-on butterfly decals on the wall. She fills the drawers and closet with Emily's clothing, and situates the yellow and green toy box under the window overlooking the duck pond. Finally, she hangs Emily's pictures—a pink ballerina, a basket full of grey kittens, and a clown riding on a circus elephant.

She carefully unfolds a Cinderella nightie and lays it on the pillow beside the Dancerella doll.

Outside of Emily's room Denita is wholly passive. She obediently comes to the table when Danny calls her for lunch and she goes to bed when he guides her into the bedroom and helps her to put on her pyjamas. He leads her outside and down to the duck pond and she watches vacantly as the Canada geese swim up to them. She will not even grant the playhouse a sideways glance.

Danny's concern grows. He knows he needs to get help for Denita but can't imagine how to go about it, given the circumstances.

He sits at the kitchen table, going over the detailed planning that they have put in place for the holiday. Everything is in order: passports for the three of them, out-of-country travel and health insurance, Disney passes, and a week of hotel reservations in Orlando for the third week of July.

The vacation will allow a much needed break for Danny between jobs. They have allowed a week for unpacking in Willow Bluff and plan to take in some of Winnipeg's summer attractions. Emily helped with the planning—the Assiniboine

Zoo was at the top of her list, followed by a cruise down the Red River on the Paddlewheel Queen. Denita has her sights set on Polo Park Mall, and Danny is excited about going to see the city's newly returned Winnipeg Goldeyes play baseball at the Stadium. And all three of them were looking forward to celebrating Canada Day at Assiniboine Park.

Danny spreads the documentation on the table and considers the options. In a leap of faith, he makes a decision. He will take Denita on the holiday after all, just the two of them. Everything is paid for. There will be nothing about the trip to remind Denita of Emily. All the memories will be new. It could prove to be what Denita needs.

As for now, Danny believes it is important that they follow their original plans. They will go on the riverboat cruise and to the baseball game and to the mall and the park. Denita will probably be unresponsive to everything but Danny knows he cannot let her slip any further into her darkness.

They will leave for the vacation right after Canada Day, as planned. Most of the luggage packing is complete; Denita took care of that last week. Danny hides Emily's bags in a spare bedroom closet and goes over the checklist Denita had prepared earlier. Everything is in perfect order.

chapter 37
Abduction

It is Canada Day. The crowd has begun to gather at Assiniboine Park by the time Danny and Denita pull into the parking lot at the zoo. Danny opens the large coloured map of the park and spreads it across the steering wheel.

"There's a duck pond just over there a ways," he says, pointing it out to Denita on the map. "Would you like to go there first?"

She nods without looking at the map. Danny helps her out of the car and they make their way across the grass to the pond. Danny buys some feed from the dispenser and gives it to Denita, hoping she will take an interest in the birds. There are several people at the pond. A dirty-looking older man lurks under the willows at the far end, and three rather ominous-looking teenagers in baggy clothing are on the other side, throwing sticks at the geese.

A young woman and a girl are walking in the direction of the seedy man and he approaches them. Danny can't hear the conversation but it is plain that the woman does not want to be part of it. She takes the girl by the hand and they walk away, closer to the pond. One of the huge ganders, obviously agitated by the stick-throwing boys, comes hissing out of the water, neck outstretched and headed directly for the little girl. Danny instinctively runs towards the child, waving his arms and making noise to distract the bird, who decides to stop its attack.

Danny can't help but notice the little girl. She is wearing a sparkly blue t-shirt and her long dark hair is pulled back in two pony tails. He sucks in a gasp. She looks enough like Emily to be a twin. Denita has noticed, too.

Danny watches the mother and child as they cross the grassy area and the parking lot to the zoo. He and Denita follow.

The zoo is crowded, and although the day is forecast to be hot, it is still pleasant enough that the animals are active. A pair of polar bears lazes in a small pool. They are putting on a show for the crowd, but Danny and Denita are focused on the dark-haired child ahead of them. The little girl laughs at the bears, and Denita whispers, "Emily."

They follow the mother and child through the big cat display, where the animals lie lethargic in the rising heat. The zoo trail leads through a wooded area and comes out at a camel enclosure. There is a camel statue there, and the little girl climbs to its back and goes down a slide.

For some reason the mother decides to go back the way they have just come, and they pass by Danny close enough that he could have reached out and touched them. They stop at the monkey cages, and Danny and Denita wait only a few feet from where they are standing. The girl waves her teddy bear towards the cage and one of the monkeys reaches through the bars as if to grab the toy.

Danny steps over and leans toward the child.

"You should stand back a bit, honey. You never know what monkeys might do." He turns to the woman. "Didn't we just see you at the duck pond?"

She laughs. "Yes, you did. You saved Nellie from the goose!"

The child smiles up at him and he smiles back. "Take care, little lady."

The woman and child stop at the concession for a drink before carrying on to the Kinsmen Discovery Centre. From there they go on to the Farmyard Barn. Danny and Denita are a little ahead of them now. Denita has come to life.

The mother and child exit the zoo through the souvenir shop and they cross back through the parking lot to a playground area where they spread out a picnic lunch and play on a big denim picnic blanket. Denita and Danny watch from a park bench in the shade on the other side of the swings. They talk animatedly. They have made a decision. Denita is crying, for the first time since the accident.

The mother and little girl pack up their picnic and migrate to the station for the little train. The Evertons follow and board three cars back. The seedy man from the duck pond is on the train too. The high-pitched whistle announces the arrival back at the little station and they all disembark.

The mother holds the girl's hand protectively on the way back to their car. The three obnoxious boys from the duck pond happen to be nearby and they approach, making threatening comments.

Danny has followed them across the parking lot.

"Get the hell out of here, creeps."

The boys slink away, managing parting obscene gestures.

Danny approaches the woman. "Are you all right?"

"Yes," she nods. "Thank you for helping. Again."

The child peers around her mother, frightened. Danny pats her on the head.

"You ok, sweetie?"

Danny and Denita hurry to their red Subaru station wagon and follow the mother and child to another parking lot near the conservatory. Hanging back, they shadow them to a large grassy area where there is an open stage. Danny decides they should keep a small distance between them. He is not sure what direction things will take, but he wants to be ready.

They follow the child to the sing-along at the stage, to the face-painting booth, to an ice cream wagon, and finally to a huge orange and blue bouncy castle. While the child is waiting in the long queue Danny and Denita evaluate the ride, looking for vulnerable spots. They find one. It is perfect.

Danny stops at a Chinese restaurant for takeout and they arrive back at the house in Willow Bluff after six. The child has not stopped crying and she convulses with hiccups. Her tears carve pink pathways through the blue face paint on her cheeks. Denita wants to wash it off but the child screams and covers her face. She refuses to eat. Finally she falls into a fitful shuddering sleep on Emily's bed, covered with the Disney Princess comforter.

Danny and Denita pack the remains of the Chinese food back into the cartons. They face each other across the kitchen table, grasping the enormity of what they have done.

"How can we possibly get away with this, Danny?" Denita covers her face with her hands. "What will we do now?"

"She looks so much like Emily, they could be twins. The long dark hair, the blue eyes, the size, everything. She's the right age…"

"But Danny, people will be looking for her. There'll be posters, searches. They'll recognize her."

"I've thought about all this, Denita. We have Emily's passport and birth certificate, those are our trump cards. We're going away for a few weeks. And by the time we get back the worst of it will have blown over."

"What will we tell people about her?"

"The same things we would have told them about Emily. In Saskatoon there might have been a few people who would see the difference, but we've left those people behind us. We don't have to worry about relatives, my parents are gone. And when's the last time you saw your parents? Have you even sent them a picture since Emily was a baby?"

"But what will we tell her? How will we explain what we did?"

"We'll start by telling her how much we love her. We can convince her that her mother asked us to take her, that she couldn't keep her any more. We can convince her that we weren't strangers. After all, how many times did we interact with them at the park?"

"What if someone finds out and they take her away from us? What if she tells someone?"

"She's really young, Denita. The first few days will be the worst. We'll have to watch her every move. Once we get to Toronto and the big zoo and Niagara Falls, she won't be able to help having some fun. By the time she gets to Disney World, she'll be healing. And by the time we get home, she'll be adjusted to us. She'll forget quickly."

Danny retrieves Emily's yellow Disney Princess luggage from the closet in the spare bedroom and places it with their bags at the front door.

They are ready to go.

Twenty Years Later

Childhood Amnesia

*Well-documented research has shown that
very little is remembered of early childhood.*

*Few adults can remember much of anything that hap-
pened to them before the age of three or four, and
only scattered incidents before the age of seven.*

*There may be snippets of memory, fleeting visions of
random events, or fragments of recollection, often
with no context as to time or place.*

*It can be difficult to determine whether these memories
are real and true, or whether they are "remembered"
because they have been told to the person or perhaps
seen in photographs.*

*Childhood amnesia was first formally reported
by psychologist Caroline Miles in 1893
in an article published in the
American Journal of Psychology.*

chapter 38
Revelation

Emily Everton picks up a couple of *People* magazines and the latest issue of *Winnipeg Free Press* from the table in the dentist's reception room. She is prepared for the usual wait and settles back with her reading material to pass the time. She thumbs through the vacuous content of the magazines first and sets them aside. She unfolds the newspaper.

The colour photograph on the front page seizes her attention. The blue-eyed child in the picture smiles widely in front of a background of bright butterflies in a garden. Her long dark hair curls to her shoulders. She is wearing a light turquoise v-neck top and a small silver butterfly-shaped locket rests below her throat. But there is something else about the photo. A red teddy bear nestles in the crook of the child's arm.

Bobby Sperling. The name pushes up, unbidden. *Why would that come to me out of nowhere?* Emily studies the photograph.

Bobby Sperling. That's the name of the bear. Emily holds the newspaper at arm's length. *But how could I possibly know that?*

She narrows her eyes and tries to bring the picture into better focus, but the newspaper definition is not precise. She can tell there are tan pads on the soles of the bear's feet, can make out the black button eyes and the shiny embroidered nose. The bear is posed with one paw on the back of the girl's arm. Emily feels a strange sensation of the plush red softness of the stuffed body. *Bobby Sperling. That's Bobby Sperling.*

But that's not all.

Emily has had a butterfly-shaped locket ever since she can remember.

She studies the picture closely. There is something about the butterfly background that is somehow familiar. She closes her eyes and visualizes wallpaper in a small bedroom: butterflies and flowers against a blue summer-clouded sky.

Emily fights to breathe. The air feels hot and thick and resistant. She struggles to understand the significance of the photograph and the newspaper account.

I'm twenty-four years old. I don't know how I know this, but I had a red teddy bear called Bobby Sperling. And I have a tiny silver butterfly locket.

For the first time she looks at the headline above the photo.

Foreboding presses in on her and she wants to put the paper down but she cannot. It is required reading.

Nellie St. Clair Kidnapping File Still Open after Twenty Years

Nellie St. Clair was only four years old when she was abducted from Assiniboine Park in Winnipeg on Canada Day twenty years ago this month.

Nellie was last seen inside a bouncy-ride play castle shortly after three in the afternoon. She was wearing a bright blue t-shirt with a pink and purple butterfly design on the front and navy shorts when she disappeared.

Nellie's face was painted with a large blue butterfly with silver sparkles. She had a long swatch of synthetic blue hair in one of her two ponytails, and she was barefoot. The four-year-old entered the castle with two slightly older girls who had waited with her in the lineup. Parents watched their children play through a large plastic window in the castle. The two older girls exited the bouncy ride on a slide a few minutes later. But Nellie never came down the slide. She seemed to have vanished in plain sight.

Two days after Nellie's disappearance, a puzzling 911 call was traced to a small restaurant near Kenora, Ontario. A faint child's voice was thought to have said, "This is Nellie," before hanging up. Nellie's mother was certain that the voice was her daughter's. The restaurant, Aunt Maggie's Truck Stop, is generally believed to have been Nellie's last known whereabouts.

Immediately following Nellie's disappearance, a massive search of Assiniboine Park, including the Assiniboine River, turned up no meaningful evidence. Volunteers plastered Winnipeg, southern Manitoba, and northwestern Ontario with posters. Thousands of leads and supposed sightings were investigated at the time of the girl's disappearance.

Nellie's abduction launched one of the largest joint police investigations in Canadian history. Initially undertaken by the City of Winnipeg Police, the case was soon taken over by the RCMP.

"We've never even come close to considering it a cold case," said RCMP Sgt. David Michales. "It's still an

active investigation and our officers continue to work on it every day."

Michales said they still receive a number of tips about this case, and everything is examined thoroughly. Over the years, police have released several composite sketches to show what Nellie St. Clair might have looked like as she grew older. Nellie would now be twenty-four years old.

"The only thing that will ever make us decide to close this case is finding Nellie," said Michales. "You never know. Somewhere out there is one small detail that can solve this mystery.

Emily fights to breathe. The air around her feels hot and thick and syrupy. The headline above the photo wavers in her vision.

There is more. The bottom third of the page features a short interview with Janelle St. Clair-Howell. She is pictured holding a red teddy bear and a photo of Nellie.

Family of Nellie St. Clair Still Hopeful

Janelle St. Clair-Howell has not seen her daughter Nellie in twenty years. The four-year-old was abducted in broad daylight from a Canada Day celebration in Winnipeg's Assiniboine Park.

The intense investigation into her disappearance turned up virtually no usable leads, except for a telephone call believed to have been made by Nellie from Kenora, Ontario.

"Yes, I listened to the tape of the 911 call," says St. Clair-Howell. "I have not a doubt in the world that it was Nellie."

Police and RCMP across Canada have always collaborated closely on the case. There were many reported sightings, especially in the months following the kidnapping, and all were thoroughly explored at the time.

St. Clair-Howell has kept many of Nellie's things. She holds the red teddy bear to her chest.

"But I don't dwell on them," she says. "Life has gone on, and we have to live each day as well as we can."

"We've never given up hope. We've never stopped searching. I've always had a strong feeling that Nellie is out there somewhere and we pray every day that she will be found."

Emily struggles to understand the significance of the photograph and the newspaper accounts.

I'm twenty-four years old. I don't know how I know this, but I had a red teddy bear called Bobby Sperling. And I have a tiny silver butterfly locket.

"Emily? Emily Everton?"

Emily wills herself back to the dentist's reception area.

"Come this way, Emily," says the receptionist. "The hygienist is going to clean and scale your teeth before the dentist sees you."

The vision of the butterfly locket fades as Emily stands and gathers her handbag and telephone. She doesn't acknowledge the receptionist. She picks up her briefcase and with the newspaper still in hand, she walks out of the building.

Emily walks west on Portage Avenue and when she comes to Memorial Boulevard she turns south. The Memorial Park fountain and pool sparkle in the heat of the mid-day light. She sits on a park bench in the shade of an elm tree and spreads the newspaper on her knee.

Bobby Sperling looks up from the front page. Bobby Sperling, the red teddy bear with his black button eyes and embroidered nose and tan-padded paws is perfect, except for one small detail that seems to be missing. What is the detail? How does Emily know about Bobby Sperling?

Emily is physically conscious of the workings of her brain. It seems to be squeezing, compressing, struggling to place Bobby Sperling. It is searching desperately for the neural pathway that will lead to him, searching for the portal that will open to reveal memories.

And then, the small detail floats into place. It's a tiny silver star, and it lands squarely on Bobby Sperling's black nose. Emily's fingers go to her own face, and she can feel the cool sensation of wet paint. She visualizes a mirror and catches sight of a sparkling blue butterfly on her face. It is not so much a memory as a fleeting snippet, dreamlike and evasive.

But Emily's brain has isolated the portal. The doorway is Bobby Sperling himself, and the memories rush from his image and swirl around Emily.

I'm walking down a street. It's windy, dusty. I'm carrying my blanket—its name is Tickly—and I'm wrapping it around me as tight as I can, but the dust is getting into my eyes and I'm crying and I'm holding Bobby Sperling close to me to keep him warm and Tickly keeps trying to get away from me.

There are hundreds of teddy bears on a big table and I can hardly see over the edge because I'm not tall, but I see a red bear right in the middle and a lady with blue hair hands him to me and I know he is mine.

It's bedtime and I can't find Bobby Sperling and then I remember I left him in the sandbox and it's raining, raining hard, because I can hear thunder and I'm crying because Bobby Sperling will be afraid, and someone goes out to get him and when Bobby Sperling comes in he's all wet and someone wraps him in a towel so I can take him to bed.

I'm sitting on a giant stone toe. It belongs to a great stone man who has horns growing out of his head. The giant is holding something sharp and dangerous. Bobby Sperling is sitting on my knee and I hold on tight to him because it's windy and I am afraid he will fall and it's a long way to the ground.

I climb up a ladder to the top of a camel but it's not real and it has a slide going down its back and I let Bobby Sperling go down first and he lands on the ground and he gets a lot of sand in his red fur and I wrap him in a blanket, a mermaid blanket, so he won't be in trouble for getting dirty.

We are on a train, a little train with no windows, just big red seats, and the whistle is blowing and I'm holding on to Bobby Sperling really tight because there is a scary man on the train and he keeps looking at me and I'm afraid he will take Bobby away from me.

"I really do remember," Emily whispers. "Bobby Sperling is *not* a figment of my imagination."

But the memories are somehow separate from the other early scant memories of her childhood. They are a part of something in a different past, one she as yet is unable to evoke.

Emily smooths the newspaper and studies the portrait of little Nellie St. Clair. Something else there is important. There is a silver butterfly necklace around the child's neck. It is a tangible link to the past. Emily still owns that little necklace. It is stored in a green Tic Tac container in her jewellery box.

The truth is both dark and shining at the same time, and it is overwhelming. There is no doubt. Emily Everton is Nellie St. Clair.

chapter 39
Photographic Memory

Emily Everton huddles at the back of the elevator on the ride up to her high-rise apartment on downtown Portage Avenue. She fights the urge to cover her face, to conceal her identity. *But how do you conceal an identity that isn't yours? Whose identity is it, after all these years?*

She steps off at the sixteenth floor in front of a middle-aged couple entering the elevator. Emily recognizes them as the tenants who live four doors down the hall from her apartment. Instinctively she puts her hand to her face. *They would almost certainly remember the incident.*

Relief and dread in equal measure fall around her as she unlocks the door and eases into the semi-darkness of her suite. She checks her mail slot and gathers a couple of letters which she tosses on the kitchen table beside her briefcase.

She pours herself a glass of Chianti, kicks off her shoes, and goes to sit on the wicker loveseat on her balcony. From here she can see Portage Avenue stretching to the west, alive with early Saturday evening traffic. Here she feels safe, anonymous.

She brings with her a hefty scrapbook album from the shelf under the coffee table. The album was given to her by her parents on the occasion of her university graduation. It delineates the history of her life in immutable terms. The photos begin in the hospital in Saskatoon right after her birth, and mark the passage of years up until her graduation.

The album is a textbook of her life experience. It goes back further than she can remember, but she recognizes every picture, every milestone, every event. She thinks of the countless times she cuddled between her parents, secure in her history as each picture and souvenir was talked about and explained.

That's your Auntie Marcy in Saskatoon. She was the very first person to see you when you were born, after Mommy and Daddy. See the beautiful pink blanket she brought you for a being-born gift? This is Mommy holding you at a baby shower at Auntie Marcy's house.

This is a picture of Daddy pushing you in your new stroller at the mall when you were three months old. And this is you with Mommy and Daddy at the park down by the river.

Look at this one, Emily! It's your first birthday! You had a chocolate cake, and we let you have it on your high chair tray. Isn't that funny? You even had chocolate icing in your hair.

She has looked at the scrapbook hundreds of times but she has never seen it as she sees it now. She searches intensely for clues and information. She already knows the truth, now she needs the proof.

The beautifully-constructed pages document the first twenty-two years of Emily's existence. Meticulously dated and captioned, it is a testament to the privileged life she has been given by Danny and Denita Everton.

Brownie badges, ballet lessons, gymnastics awards, piano recitals, figure skating and ringette, swimming and soccer, and downhill skiing in the mountains—there is seemingly no end to the opportunities Emily has enjoyed.

And the family has travelled. There are early pictures of Emily at the Toronto Zoo and Niagara Falls and in front of the Magic Castle at Disney World. In her teens she stands at the top of a black diamond run on Whistler. She waves at the presidents' stone faces at the Black Hills. She suns on a beach in Barbados.

She goes through the scrapbook again from the beginning, trying to find a time-point where she can differentiate real memories from those that have been implanted by repetition. She forces her mind to dig through the layers. There is very little available true recollection until about age nine, she decides.

The most interesting discovery is that there are many memories that are not represented in the scrapbook. There are recollections of a bad fall from a tricycle that left her bleeding from a deep cut on her elbow, a sleepover at her friend Cindy's birthday party when she was seven, being covered in swimmers' rash from Rock Lake the summer she lost her front teeth.

In particular, Emily remembers visiting Disney World when she was thirteen. At the time she was unable to explain the profound sadness that surrounded her there.

And then there is the red teddy bear Bobby Sperling, who is conspicuously absent from the scrapbook.

Emily spreads the paper beside the scrapbook. She studies the portrait of Nellie St. Clair and compares it to pictures of herself taken twenty years ago.

Right before the holiday photos of Toronto and Niagara and Disney World, there are several pictures of Emily playing on top of a large packing crate in the living room of the Saskatoon house where they lived before moving to Winnipeg. She appears to have a colouring book spread in front of her. A Dancerella doll sits between her legs. Her dark shoulder length hair frames her face and she peers cutely from beneath wispy bangs. In the immediate next series of pictures, the family is at the zoo in Toronto, and then at Niagara Falls. Emily is standing in front of the monkey cages. Her long hair is pulled back in two pony tails. There are no wispy bangs.

Emily has found the time-point.

She throws the scrap book across the room and it breaks open and the pages spread across the carpet like an oversized deck of cards.

It's nothing more than a beautiful work of fiction. I'm nothing but a work of fiction. So where is the real Emily Everton?

She tries to put the scrapbook together. The rings are sprung and will not close. There is no way to reassemble the pages in order.

She reclines in her balcony loveseat high over Portage Avenue and watches the perpetual river of taillights flow away toward the sunset. It is eerily quiet up here, save for the occasional police or ambulance siren.

Nellie St. Clair. I'm Nellie St. Clair.

chapter 40
Goodbye, Emily

Annoyed, Danny Everton digs the Saturday edition of the Winnipeg Free Press out of the lilacs beside the front step. *Why the hell can't the kid manage to land it on the porch? Just once?* He takes the paper to the porch swing where he relaxes in the July breeze.

He sips his coffee and opens the paper. The entire front page is devoted to the twentieth anniversary of an unsolved child abduction.

NELLIE ST. CLAIR KIDNAPPING FILE
STILL OPEN AFTER TWENTY YEARS

Centred on the page is a portrait of a dark-haired child holding a red teddy bear.

Danny knows the story by heart. His collection of faithfully saved clippings, still hidden in an old sports bag in the basement, documents the original kidnapping and the initial frantic search and investigation. For the first few years, coverage of the disappearance of little Nellie St. Clair surfaced regularly around

Canada Day, but as time passed the investigation seemed to wane. Still, Danny watches vigilantly for even the tiniest of updates.

Danny removes the front page to add to the collection in the dusty sports bag. He tosses the rest of the newspaper in the trash bin. There is no point in taking the chance that Denita might see it, even after all these years. If she asks about the paper, he will tell her it wasn't delivered. It is important to shield Denita from any reference to the abduction. She has somehow managed a complete suppression of the event. Sometimes Danny wishes he had been able to do the same.

He goes into the house to finish reading the paper. There is another small story in the second section of the paper in a sidebar devoted to *Cross-Canada News*. It catches his eye because it is from Saskatoon.

> **Saskatoon**—*Construction crews preparing a site for a new bridge on the Anger Lake Road north of Saskatoon discovered the remains of a child last week. Local RCMP estimate the remains have probably been under the bridge for at least twenty years. The sex of the child is unknown at this point and there have been no historical reports of missing children in the area. The investigation is continuing, and will include DNA and dental comparisons, said RCMP.*

Danny has been completely focused on protecting Denita over the years. He has paid little attention to his own suppressed demons. Now, a black dreadfulness engulfs his mind.

He forces himself to enter the memory. It is all storybook happiness at first, but he knows where it will lead. He doesn't want to follow, but the pull of the past is too powerful.

Danny was on his way home after his last day of work at the Westridge Heights Inn. A box of Chinese takeout sat beside him on the passenger seat of the Subaru Station wagon. He was hungry and tired and in a hurry, looking forward to the last meal in the house with Denita and Emily. They all loved Chinese food. The aroma of the meal was mouthwatering and filled the car. There were cartons of pineapple pork with fried rice and shrimp chop suey, vegetable stir fry and spring rolls, and chicken balls with sticky red sauce, Emily's favorite.

He was thinking as he drove about some final details of packing that needed to be taken care of before settling in for the last night in Saskatoon. He pictured the fire he was going to light in the fireplace with a firelog he had saved for the occasion. They would eat the Chinese food and enjoy a bottle of wine Denita had put aside. They planned to sleep in the double sleeping bag on the futon and Emily would be in her own little pink and purple bag on the floor beside them. He smiled, thinking of how excited Emily was about these "picnic in the house" plans.

Danny was running late and the weather wasn't helping. Heavy rain and wind pushed in from the west in a sudden prairie thunderstorm and the windshield wipers were thunking at top speed to clear the sheets of water from the windshield. He checked the clock on the dash. It read just past seven and he remembered thinking how weirdly dark it was for the end of June and he hoped Denita wouldn't be worrying. The city street lights flickered on and off and on and off before they died. He could feel the slip of the tires as he hydroplaned the station wagon around the cul-de-sac and into the driveway. Out of habit he pressed the remote door opener on his visor. The garage door didn't engage and he remembered there was no electricity.

The only light was coming from the Subaru's headlights. Danny could see something dark against the garage door—a strange meaningless shape. He instinctively sensed the wrongness of the dark mass. He realized it was Denita. He jumped out of the car and the wind took the door hard on its hinges and it slammed him on the knee. Denita was crouched over and he could see that she was trying to shield something from the gusting rain. He knelt beside her and tried to lift her to her feet.

He had no sense of how long he stooped over her in the driving rain. It was probably only a few seconds, but it was one of those moments that stretched out in agonizing slow motion. And in that moment he comprehended the unspeakable horror in Denita's lap.

He barged into the garage through the open side door and stumbled past the rows and piles of packing boxes. Outside, the storm thundered and lit up the sky in jagged strobes. Inside, it was black except for the sputtering weak light from a flashlight on the floor. He could make out the tall ladder standing in the middle of the garage, and the red handle for the manual operation of the door dangling just above it. He climbed the ladder and with herculean strength managed to wrench down the cord and hoist up the heavy door. The cord ripped the skin from the palms of his hands but he felt no pain and was not aware of the warm blood trickling down his wrist. He locked the lever back into the chain.

He staggered back outside and fell to his knees on the pavement and lifted Denita and Emily into his arms. The rain lashed at the three of them and blood washed away down the driveway in diluted red streams. Danny wasn't sure of how long they huddled there. He began to shiver. He pried Denita away from Emily and lifted the broken little body and held it to his chest. He remembered the keening howl that tore from his throat and how it was silenced by the wind and the rain and the thunder.

The electricity flickered on—a dim brown at first which evolved to yellow and finally ignited everything in a blaze of cruel brightness.

He could feel the softness of Emily. She was cold and limp and soaking wet against his chest. He forced himself to look at the dear little *face. Her eyes were half open and empty and her mouth formed a tiny O, as if she was trying to say something.*

Denita remained unmoving, sitting cross-legged on the driveway, staring at her lap as if there was still something there.

The car's headlights and the lights in the garage now shone against each other and in the cross-shadows Danny remembered thinking everything looked like a scene from a Stephen King movie.

His mind raced and measured and tried to arrive at a plan. Decision-making. That's what he was good at. But there wasn't much time. There wasn't much time…

He dragged a green plaid car blanket from the back seat of the station wagon and wrapped it around Emily like a cocoon and carried her to the car.

Denita still wasn't moving. He knew he had to get her inside before he left. He dragged her to her feet and she felt like a dead-weight sleeping child as he carried her into the house. He dug a couple of Valiums out of her purse on the counter and she managed to swallow them with a glass of white wine from the bottle they intended to have with the Chinese food. He laid her on the futon where they had planned to sleep and covered her with the big double sleeping bag. He turned off all the lights.

He found a big blue tarp behind one of the packing boxes in the garage and rolled it up tight and took it to the car. He closed the garage door with the remote and backed out of the driveway into the rain. The downpour was now, if anything, heavier than before. The driver's side door refused to close completely. Something had been bent when the wind forced it out of his grip earlier and little splashes of rain now drove in through the crack.

Danny thought he had been driving for hours. For some reason the dash lights had dimmed and he couldn't see the clock. There was almost no traffic on the highway, and he had no idea where he was. Thoughts of little Evan filled his mind, and of how he had died in his crib. Denita had been hysterical for days after that. She never stopped blaming herself even though everyone said it wasn't her fault. But Danny remembered the way the Family Services people harassed her. At least, that was how Denita interpreted it at the time. She was too fragile to go through that again. She would surely be blamed for Emily's death, perhaps even charged, Danny reasoned.

But there was another way.

He drove out into the wide country north of Saskatoon and finally knew where he was, as the sign said *Anger Lake Road*. The gas gauge registered below a quarter tank. He had filled it up for the trip to Winnipeg the next day and now found himself hoping he would have enough gas to get home.

There was an old wooden bridge just ahead. Danny pulled onto the soggy gravel shoulder of the road and stopped at the bridge. This would be the place.

He was gentle with Emily, as if he was afraid to awaken her. He folded the blue tarp around her in a protective shroud. He pushed the compact little bundle against the embankment on the underside of the bridge and as far up into the dry space as he could reach.

It was still raining, and the wind was stronger than ever. He returned to the car. The Chinese food on the passenger seat was cold and its smell was sickening. He threw the box into a nearby ditch.

Danny couldn't recall the drive back to the city. When he got home Denita was sleeping exactly as he had left her. He was wet and shivering and he crawled under the big sleeping bag beside her and gently cradled her chilled body.

It was over.

chapter 41
Confrontation

The Everton home in Willow Bluff has aged beautifully over the past twenty years. Denita's masterful landscaping has matured into a shady park-like setting and the house with its new windows looks better, if possible, than when it was new. A vine-covered pergola shades a small circular patio where the ginger-bread playhouse used to be, and a terraced pond nearby teems with large goldfish. The duck pond hasn't changed much, except that is it now in danger of being overrun by Canada geese.

Emily pulls into the circular front drive and gathers her broken scrapbook into her arms. She has not told them she is coming but that is not at all unusual, as she often stops in on Sunday morning for coffee and brunch. She finds them in the shade of the pergola.

Denita rises to meet her.

"Hi, sweetie. You're just in time for coffee and croissants."

Danny pulls out a chair for her and motions for her to sit down. He pushes a plate of croissants and a carousel of jam in her direction.

"I'm sorry. I can't stay. I just have to talk to you about something."

Danny and Denita exchange glances.

"Is everything all right?" Danny asks.

"No. It isn't."

"What's the matter, sweetie?" asks Denita. "What's wrong?" Her eyes take in the fractured scrapbook. "Oh dear, Emily, what's happened?"

Emily has been rehearsing the conversation in her mind since last night. She is going to be calm and reasonable. She is going to wait patiently for the painful explanation. She is not going to get angry.

The words refuse to come out the way she had planned them. She dumps the scrapbook on the glass table, scattering a pile of yellow napkins to the stone patio.

"Can you explain this to me?"

Danny grabs the pages to keep them from sliding off the table.

"What the heck are you talking about? What happened to the album? Calm down, Emily. Tell us what's going on."

"I'm pretty certain you know exactly what's going on. And it's been going on for twenty years."

Denita opens her mouth to say something but Emily interrupts before she can make a sound.

"I'm not Emily Everton. I'm Nellie St. Clair."

Denita sucks in a gasp. "Don't be ridiculous, Emily. Whatever would make you say something like that?"

Emily shuffles through the sheets. Her hands are sweaty and shaking. She holds out four pages. The first two are filled with pictures and commentary of the family's last few days in Saskatoon. The next pages document a trip to southern Ontario and Disney world.

"Have a close look, Mom and Dad."

"You've seen these pictures hundreds of times, Emily," Danny says. "What are you getting at?"

"Look at my hair in the pictures, Dad. There I am, playing on a pile of packing boxes in our house in Saskatoon. That had to have been only a couple of days before we left. I have bangs in the picture, dad. Bangs."

Danny and Denita share a look of confusion.

"And now look at these pictures of me in front of the Magic Castle in Disney World. My hair is longer, and I don't have bangs."

"That doesn't mean a thing," Denita says. "It's just the way it's tied back in those ponytails".

"It does mean something, Mom. It means that these are two different girls. Hair just doesn't grow two or three inches in a few days."

Danny senses the imminent collapse of everything he has worked so hard to protect.

"You took me from my real mother. From my home and from God knows what else. Do I have grandparents? Aunts and uncles and cousins? Where are they, right here in Winnipeg? Right under my nose all these years? How could you take all that away from me?"

"What did we take away, Emily? We gave you the best life a child could have. We gave you our unconditional love."

"What about my real mother's love?"

Denita has stopped crying.

"I'm your real mother, Emily. You're our daughter. Nothing can ever change that."

Emily extracts the Saturday newspaper from her handbag.

"Well then, what about this?" She spreads the front page on top of the croissants.

Denita has not seen the newspaper, and it takes a few moments for the story to sink in.

Danny can feel the palpitations of his heart escalating almost to the point of being audible. He feels dizzy. The duck pond looks like an ocean, and he is seasick. He cannot speak.

"It's all some kind of a mistake," says Denita. "There's absolutely no way that could be you."

Emily reaches into the depths of her purse and comes up with a green Tic Tac container. She spills the contents into the palm of her hand. The tiny silver butterfly necklace sparkles in the sunlight. Emily lays the necklace on top of the portrait of Nellie St. Clair. It is undeniably one and the same

chapter 42
Denouement

Danny and Denita call several times a day but Emily refuses to answer the telephone. She ignores the doorbell and has instructed her assistant at work to tell them she is out. She will be ready to see them someday soon, but not now.

She spends hours researching the St. Clair-Howell family. They have lived in the same pink stucco bungalow in St. James for over twenty years. *I'm pretty sure I remember that house. Pink. And didn't it have a veranda?* They have two teenage sons, Michael and Mark. *My half-brothers!* Janelle St. Clair-Howell works for an accounting firm in downtown Winnipeg. *Four blocks from my apartment.* Jamie Howell has his own successful detective agency, specializing in missing children.

She deliberates for a week without arriving at a decision. There is no one to whom to turn for advice. Ramifications pile upon ramifications in her mind. No matter what she chooses to do, there will be both happiness and sadness.

Denita and Danny have been exemplary parents. *They've given me a privileged life.* There has never been any doubt of their love. *I'll always love them. They've sacrificed everything for me.* What will happen to them now? Will the St. Clair-Howells press charges after all this time?

And what about Janelle St. Clair-Howell? How will she react after all these years? *Will she believe me?* What was it that she said in the newspaper article?

"We've never given up hope. We've never stopped searching."

She'll undoubtedly meet me with open arms. It'll be a wonderful, tearful reunion. They'll want to know all about my life without them. Will they be satisfied with getting to know me gradually or will they want me to come and live with them? What will my brothers think of me?

But who will I be? My whole life has centred around my identity as Emily Everton. How can I just strip that away and move forward as if it never happened? I know I can't ever become the Nellie that was taken. But I will never really be Emily again, either.

Emily sits in her car across the street from the neat corner-lot bungalow. Past the low privacy fence she can see a small cedar deck and a glass-topped patio table with a red umbrella. Neat flower beds circle the perimeter of the yard. A basketball hoop juts from the front of the single car garage, and a bicycle leans against the front step. Red and white petunias cascade from window boxes around the veranda.

Emily is clutching the tiny silver butterfly necklace. She opens her hand. She spreads the necklace over the newspaper picture of Nellie and Bobby Sperling for one final verification. There is absolutely no doubt.

She gathers the scrapbook pages which she has managed to return to a semblance of order. She has separated the pages for the first four and a half years from the rest. She folds the newspaper story so Nellie's photograph is on top. Necklace in hand,

MARGARET RIDDELL

she gets out of her car and crosses the street in the direction of the pink stucco bungalow.

Printed in Canada